HER PROTECTOR

Boston Doms Book Three

JANE HENRY
MAISY ARCHER

Published by Blushing Books
An Imprint of
ABCD Graphics and Design, Inc.
A Virginia Corporation
977 Seminole Trail #233
Charlottesville, VA 22901

©2019
All rights reserved.

No part of the book may be reproduced or transmitted in any form or by any means, electronic or mechanical, including photocopying, recording, or by any information storage and retrieval system, without permission in writing from the publisher. The trademark Blushing Books is pending in the US Patent and Trademark Office.

Jane Henry and Maisy Archer
Her Protector, Boston Doms Book Three

EBook ISBN: 978-1-68259-821-4
Print ISBN: 978-1-64563-161-3
v1

Cover Art by ABCD Graphics & Design
This book contains fantasy themes appropriate for mature readers only. Nothing in this book should be interpreted as Blushing Books' or the author's advocating any non-consensual sexual activity.

Chapter 1

Tessa watched as the teen-aged boys drying off her car wiped their towels over the hood in rhythmic circles. Over and over again, the flashes of brilliant white moved until her car gleamed like a polished sapphire in the sunlight. The tallest boy with a towel stepped back and gave her a thumb's up. She nodded her thanks and pulled into the busy intersection of Main and Hawthorne Street, grateful that her car, at least, would not draw any attention from anyone. That was exactly what she needed. Anonymity.

No one needed to see that all her worldly possessions were stuffed in the back of her car.

Her first stop would be The Club, the Boston BDSM club so well known and well-respected that it had ceased to be known by any other name, where she could sneak in a quick shower. *Sneak* being the operative word. Though Tessa had been a frequent visitor to The Club for a long while, this was well outside of business hours for anyone but the daily cleaning crew, who tended to leave the basement door open while they worked. Unfortunately, she had nowhere else to shower. And sneaking in wasn't exactly breaking and entering, was it?

She wasn't sure her friends would agree. Tessa's boss, Tony Angelico, had a brother named Matteo who *worked* at The Club, and Tessa knew that if Matteo found out she went to The Club without permission; he'd have to tell Tony. And Matteo's girlfriend Hillary was one of the few friends Tessa had. Tessa would die of mortification if anyone found out she was here. Stealth was crucial.

Tessa let herself into the basement stock room, then quickly ran up the short flight of stairs to where the employee changing rooms and facilities were. Tessa was not a sneaky person, and letting herself into The Club left her feeling queasy and uncomfortable. But she was experienced at being stealthy. When one grew up with a mom like she did, one grew accustomed to slipping about unseen.

Thirty minutes later, Tessa pulled her clean car into the parking lot of *Cara*, the restaurant where she worked as both event coordinator and manager. She thought how easy it was for the well to do to take cleanliness for granted. Access to hot water, showers and a place to brush her teeth was something Tessa did not take for granted, and she took a minute to mourn the loss of the apartment she'd tried so desperately to claim as her very own.

Sunday would've been her move-in date. After so many years of working hard and saving every penny, living in the dismal house she'd grown up in so that her sister Nora wouldn't have to take care of their mother alone, keeping her mother's electricity on and the refrigerator stocked, she'd thought she could finally have a place to herself, a place to call home. The only reason she'd stayed so long at the dismal apartment she'd grown up in was because she couldn't imagine leaving her sister alone. The plan was that once Nora hit her eighteenth birthday in just a few months, she'd move in with Tessa.

She'd finally made her way, finally had enough saved. The landlord required first month's rent, last month's rent and a security deposit. Hillary had put in a good word for her, and Tessa was moving in to a two-bedroom apartment nearby. The money had been socked away and untouched. But things hadn't gone as planned.

Nora had called.

Tessa sighed, as she parked her car and took the keys out of her ignition.

One day, things would change. In many ways, they already had. She had already made her way in the professional world, establishing herself as dependable and hardworking, and Tony was pleased with the work that she did. She was paid well, and things were looking up.

But damn it all, if she didn't always seem to take two steps forward and one step back.

How could she use the money she'd saved for an apartment when Nora needed her? Every penny she'd given Nora to pay for the books she needed for school had been found by her mother, who'd gone on a drinking spree and spent every damn penny. Nora needed the money, and she needed it *now*.

But Tessa would be damned if she'd beg her mother to let her move back in, either. Not after she'd angered her by saying she was moving out in the first place.

Glancing in the mirror, Tessa took a long, appraising look at the bags under her eyes, and her freshly-washed hair that was now almost dry, but stuck up in various odds and ends like a bale of hay. She sighed. She loved her auburn tresses, but really needed to touch up her hair and make-up before everyone else came to work. Her small overnight bag with make-up and hair accessories was tucked under her desk in her office, and no one usually showed up at *Cara* until noon, even Tony, as he pulled a late shift frequently. Tessa's stomach growled, and she groaned. Damn it. She'd forgotten breakfast *again*.

She smoothed a hand over her skirt, thankful she'd found the little dress at the consignment shop at Downtown Crossing.

Living in Boston had decided perks. Sure, it could be really pricey if you mingled with the yuppies and drank five-dollar lattes with your seven-dollar scones. But Boston was home to droves of college students, and second-hand clothing stores, consignment shops and discount stores were abundant, if you just knew where to look.

And Tessa knew where to look.

She'd scored the olive-green wrap dress, a casual little number made of cotton and polyester that wouldn't wrinkle no matter how she twisted it, for just a few dollars. The manager had put it behind the counter for her, insisting she try it on when she came for the Saturday morning perusal.

"It's you," she'd insisted. "Babe. You don't even need to try it on. Fork over the four bucks and take her home." She *had* tried it on, of course. And it *had* been her, as if it had been cut and sized to order. It dipped into a low vee in the front, just low enough to show off her ample assets, but not too low it was indecent. The empire waist accentuated her top but flared enough to make her look curvy, and not, as her mother always said, "dumpy and fat."

Tessa was a curvy girl, and it was one reason she'd been drawn to The Club to begin with. Her ex, a former employee of The Club, told her "kinky guys like curvy chicks." She still wasn't sure if it were true, but it sure felt nice to believe it. For sure, the girls at The Club weren't all supermodels. Hillary was thin and gorgeous, but her sister Heidi was all Marilyn-Monroe-like curves. Alice, the woman who tended bar but liked to play, was lovely but no waif either. Tessa felt like she fit in with these girls. As she pulled her purse from the backseat, glancing every which way in the parking lot to make sure no one was coming, she thought of Tony's ex-girlfriend, Val. Always dressed to the nines, with perfectly manicured nails and flawless makeup, Val looked like she could've stepped off a runway. Val would've died a thousand deaths before she bought make-up at the local drug store, rather than a high-end department store. She wouldn't have purchased a second-hand dress if someone put a gun to her head. And the thought of sleeping overnight in her car...

Tessa shook her head. Why start the day thinking about the bitch who'd held the staff at *Cara* hostage with her temper, sharp tongue and control over Tony? Val was history. And sure, Tessa couldn't compare, but just maybe she didn't *need* to.

It was hard not to compare, though. Val had landed Tony—for a time, yes, but still. She'd been *Tony's*. Tessa sighed.

God, she had to get her shit together.

Opening the employee entrance, Tessa stepped in quickly, and glanced around to make sure no one else was there yet. Scanning the parking lot wasn't always reliable, as not everyone drove their own car. Occasionally, someone was there early when deliveries were made, or a big event was imminent, but the place looked vacant. She exhaled. She hadn't realized she'd been holding her breath.

Her office was near Tony's, a small office to the side of the kitchen, with one thin wall between his office and hers. She'd hated that wall when Tony was dating Val. She could hear the fights they had, and suspected she heard a few other things as well. But now, she liked the fact that she could hear him on the phone during the day, or when he was talking with other employees. She liked the sound of his voice, deep and mellow, especially when he teasingly called her Miss Damon.

She reached for the light switch in the kitchen, and gasped when the light went on before she flicked the switch. Tony stood at the restaurant-entrance to the kitchen, his large frame dwarfing the doorway, blinking in surprise at her.

"Oh! Sorry, Tess. I didn't know you were there." He smiled. "You scared the hell out of me."

Her heart was still pounding in her chest, not just from having been startled, but now hearing his voice and the way he smiled, his hazel eyes crinkling at her. His dark hair was still damp as if he just got out of the shower, and he had a little dimple when he smiled at her. She smiled back. God, it was so much nicer to be around him now that Val wasn't there anymore. And then she remembered she still had hay-bale hair and a makeup-less face. She turned from him quickly.

"Morning, Tony," she said, opening the door to her office and fairly sprinting in, shutting the door behind her.

Smooth, girl. Real smooth.

She grabbed her bag with her hair straightener and make-up. Ugh. Now, how was she going to get to the bathroom to fix herself up? She didn't have a mirror in her office, and having her boss hauling her stuff to the employee bathroom wasn't part of her initial strategy. She groaned. Crap! Well, the hair would be okay tucked into a clip or something, maybe. She rummaged through her bag and found one. Running her hands through the soft, but unruly locks, she quickly tucked it into a clip and grabbed her purse. Oh! There was a little compact mirror on the top of her makeup case. She quickly applied the lightest foundation, ran a mascara brush through her eyelashes and slid lip gloss across her lips. Phew. That was better.

A knock came on the door just as she puckered her lips.

"Come in," she said.

Tony entered, and smiled at her. Tony had the Angelico-brother grin, the same deep voice and dark hair. But that was where the physical similarities to his brother Matteo and Matt's identical twin, Dom, ended. His strong jaw was clean-shaven, and he was huskier, with wide shoulders, large arms and equally large, very capable hands.

"Hey, you look nice," he said, and her belly warmed just a little. "I'm sorry I scared you when you came in."

She shrugged. "No biggie. What's up?"

He held up a paper Dunkin Donuts bag. "They accidentally gave me three muffins instead of two. I think the girl there has a thing for me. She always calls me 'honey' and winks at me. I think she's trying to butter me up."

Tessa laughed, gesturing for him to come over and sit across from her at the desk. "Honey, I think it's a prerequisite that all the girls who work that Dunks in Boston call their customers 'honey.' And yes, please. I would *love* a muffin. I forgot breakfast and I'm starving."

He grinned, laying a napkin atop her desk and arranging the muffins.

"Uh. Blueberry… pumpkin… and cranberry orange, I think?" He leaned over and sniffed, which made her giggle.

"God, I love pumpkin muffins," she groaned, reaching for it, but then she stopped. "Wait, you ordered two. Which ones did you want? I'm not gonna take yours."

He shrugged. "A muffin is a muffin is a muffin," he muttered. "Take what you want first."

"I'm not gonna take your muffin! What did you order? Is the pumpkin yours?"

He sighed. "Tess. Take any one you want."

She crossed her arms over her chest stubbornly. "No. Tell me which ones you ordered!"

He leaned over the table at her. "Infuriating girl, take whatever damn muffin you want. Wait, you said you like pumpkin?" He nabbed the pumpkin muffin and handed it to her on a napkin. "Eat."

"Tony!"

"Tessa!"

Frowning, she took the pumpkin muffin and suddenly felt self-conscious about eating it in front of him. What if he'd ordered the pumpkin?

"God, it's good to see a woman eat a muffin," he muttered, ripping the top off the blueberry and eating half of it in one ginormous bite. He swallowed. "Even if she's as stubborn as a goddamn mule."

"You should've just told me which you ordered," she muttered, taking a tiny nibble. Mmm, it was good. Spicy and sweet and still warm. She took another, larger bite.

"Well, you're the one who wanted to eat my pumpkin muffin," he said. She nearly choked.

"Oh my God!" she said, and he chuckled, sounding exactly like his brothers when he did. She shook her head, reaching for the carton under her desk for a can of Diet Coke. She popped the top and took a large swig. She hated coffee, always had, and preferred starting her day with what she called her caffeinated bubbly.

"I have no idea how you can drink that stuff with breakfast," he said with a grimace, as he sipped his coffee.

"You drink ginger ale with cannoli," she said in her defense. "That's just as weird. Except mine is caffeinated and makes more sense."

"Have you *tried* drinking ginger ale with cannoli? I highly recommend it. Don't knock it 'til you've tried it."

"Well, I'd probably eat John's cannoli with just about any drink," she admitted. Their head pastry chef, John, was a master at the craft, and the cannoli he made were creamy but not too sweet, dusted with powdered sugar, and he had some kind of a method with the shells that made them crispy and as light as air. She loved them.

Tony had already polished off his blueberry muffin and reached for the cranberry.

"Either you were starving, or that was one good muffin," she said, as she still had two thirds of hers left and he was already starting in on his second.

"It wasn't as good as a pumpkin, but I'll take it," he said, his eyes twinkling at her. "And anyway, I've gotta eat plenty of carbs to maintain my chiseled physique," he said sarcastically. He patted his belly. Though he was far from overweight, he was a good-sized guy. Tessa never had gone for the tall, lanky type. Something about Tony's large, well-padded frame made her feel small and feminine. She snorted as she intentionally took a large bite of the pumpkin muffin.

"This one's *delicious,"* she said, smacking her lips. "Just the right balance of sweet and spice." She closed her eyes and moaned, licking her lips. When she opened them again, she noticed his eyes had gone half-lidded and his Adam's apple moved up and down as he swallowed. Um, oops. She hadn't meant to make the muffin teasing into a sexual escapade. He *was,* after all, her boss, though the thought of him really being attracted to her was pretty much the best thing that happened to her all month… hell, all *year.*

She took a swig of Diet Coke, placed the muffin to the side, and sat up straighter. "So, are we all set for the Martin party this evening?"

He nodded and sat up straighter himself. "John's got the pastry sorted, Rao says the menu is ready to go, and all preparations are in full swing. Oh, and Nicole is coming early to help set up."

Rao had been promoted from wait staff to the kitchen, and Nicole was head waitress. Perfect.

"Oh, hey, I have a problem, though. Maybe you can help me?" he asked.

Hell, yeah, she could help him. Maybe he'd say something like, "I have this itch right behind my shoulder blades. Would you mind scratching?" or "My neck is really tight and maybe you can help massage out this knot…"

God, Tessa. Get a freaking grip!

"What's up?" She was eager to hear what he needed. Sure, he was her boss, and yes, he was on the rebound having broken up with Val just a few weeks before, but hell if she didn't want to get on his good side.

"My car's in the shop," he said. Ah, so that explained why it wasn't in the employee parking lot. "Matteo took me in this morning, but has to be at The Club this afternoon and can't take me to go pick up my car." Her stomach began to clench, and she had a sinking feeling as he continued. "Is there any way you can take me? It's just a few miles from here and should be ready by four, which gives me enough time to pick it up and be back here for the Martin party."

Oh, God. He wanted a *ride?* How would she hide all her stuff? She couldn't! There was too much of it. But she couldn't lie to him, either. Her passenger seat was teeming with clothes, and the back seat was literally nothing but bags and boxes.

She should tell him no. She had to come up with some excuse. But what? She couldn't tell him her car wasn't working. Duh. It was right in the employee parking lot. She didn't have plans because she had to be there for the Martin party anyway. She blinked. Shit! She was not good at thinking on her feet.

And this was a chance to do a favor for her favorite person in the entire world.

"Sure," she said helplessly, nodding, trying her very best to pretend her world wasn't imploding, and that she was so totally nonchalant about everything. She'd find a way to move her stuff before then. She would have to. "Yeah, I can take you."

He stood, flashing that Angelico brother grin that should've been outlawed. It wasn't fair what it did to a woman. She swallowed, and feigned having her shit together as she smiled back.

"Thanks, Tess," he said, brushing the crumbs off her desk and into the bag. He crumpled it up, turned to the wastebasket, bent at the knees and shot. It bounced off the rim and fell to the floor. She stood and picked it up, shooting it in the way he did, but this time, she scored.

"Show off," he muttered, shaking his head, but his eyes twinkled as he left her office.

She thought of her car filled with all her worldly possessions, as she watched his retreating figure. She slumped against the side of her desk. Tony made everything seem so simple and straightforward.

Why couldn't things be that way for her?

It was lunchtime, but she was still full from the muffin and too nervous to eat, anyway. She worked with Tony every single day, but ever since the day Val had pushed her over the edge at Heidi and Dom's rehearsal dinner, things had been different. Val had accused her of hitting on Tony, but Tessa had been nothing but professional. When Val finally mumbled the word "slut," Tessa had completely snapped, snagging a glass of red wine off the table and tossing it full force at Val. She'd met her mark completely, and was secretly pleased to see Val's furious expression accompanied by a high-pitched shriek.

Val's flip-out over that incident had pushed Tony to do what Tessa and every single member of the staff at *Cara* had wanted to do ever since Val had set her first Valentino stiletto in the door. He broke up with her. Hillary secretly gave Tessa a high-five, and John and Rao had been thrilled. They all kept their responses from Tony, however, who was brooding, but seemed somehow relieved.

Tessa wasn't sure if it was her guilty conscience or the fact that all the men she hung out with were dominants at The Club, but she had expected a stern lecture from Tony. She felt she'd deserved it. Even though Val was out of line, Tessa knew giving way to her temper never ended well for anyone. She was raised by a mother with a raging anger issue, and Tessa had a hard time controlling her anger when she was pushed. But Tony never said a word. He'd taken Val home, and the next day at the wedding, had bought her a drink.

After that drink, she and Tony had talked until the wee hours of the morning. She'd been doing her best to prove to him that she wasn't the crazy bitch who threw glasses of wine at people.

She would not do what she had done all through her teen years. No, she would not.

Her dresses and jeans always hid the scars on her thighs and she would die a thousand deaths before she would ever reveal to Tony, Hillary, or any of her friends at *Cara* or The Club that she was more than a masochist who craved spanking, but really what her mother called her regularly: *fucked up*.

Tessa shook her head. No. She had worked too damn hard to go down that rabbit trail of degradation *again*. She was *not* fucked up. Her high school guidance counselor, Mrs. Evans, would chew her out for that. Hell, even her little sister Nora would shake her head and stomp her foot and tell her not to go there. Her *mother* was the one who was fucked up. Tessa was strong, and capable, and *better than that*.

Tessa sat at her desk and lifted the edge of her dress just slightly, touching the raised scars that were the only remnants of the out-of-control girl she once was. Her hand shook slightly as she tentatively touched the deepest scar she had, the one on her left leg, the one that she'd opened up over and over again. The one that had finally caught the attention of her friend in high school, who had gone straight to Mrs. Evans. Tessa hadn't spoken to her friend for months over that. But it was the turning point in her life.

She shoved her dress down and pushed to her feet, just as a knock came on her office door.

"Come in!" she yelled. She typically kept her office door open, but today she'd needed some privacy. The door opened, and Hillary stepped in.

God, Hillary looked amazing. She was always cute, and so pixie-like Matteo had nicknamed her "Tinker Bell." But now she fairly glowed.

"Hey, babe," Hillary said cheerfully, stepping into the office. "What's up?"

"Oh, I was just stepping out for a few minutes," Tessa said.

"Need to run a few errands." Her few errands involved finding a place to shove all the belongings that were littering her car so Tony could find a place to sit.

"You wanna go grab some lunch?" Hill asked, and Tessa shook her head.

"Sorry, not today, Hill. Got too much to do. How are you and Matt doing?"

Hillary flushed and lowered her eyes. Tessa giggled. That was a good sign.

"Oh my gosh," Hillary whispered. "Amazing! And I finally got the rest of my stuff moved into his place this weekend. Well, I should say *he* got it moved in because you know the Angelico brothers. He was all, 'Don't lift a thing,'" she said, in a deep voice that sounded familiar. Tessa giggled, as Hillary continued her imitation. "*I'm* the one who carries the heavy shit. You go get the towels."

Tessa smirked, but looked over Hillary's shoulder and widened her eyes. "Oh, hi, Matteo," she said. "We were just talking about you!"

Hillary gasped and swirled around, as Tessa burst into laughter.

Hillary turned back to Tessa, her eyes narrowed and her cheeks flushed. "Oh my God," she hissed. "I am *so* gonna get you —" but she was silenced, as Matteo came up behind her and wrapped strong arms around her.

"Hey, babe," he said, as he waved to Tessa. "S'up, Tess."

Tessa waved back, slinging her bag over her shoulder. "What's up, Matt? Hoping to catch some of Rao's tortellini before you hit The Club?"

Matteo shook his head as his eyes danced. "Am I that predictable?"

"Yes," said both girls in unison.

He gave Hillary a teasing swat and waved a finger at Tessa. "You two watch it," he said warningly, and Tessa merely stuck her tongue out at him. Though Matteo occasionally played the role of Dungeon Master at The Club, Tessa had strategically made sure she never ended up playing a scene when he was around. It was just too weird at work. He knew she went, and he was friendlier to her than ever at The Club since Val outed her at the rehearsal dinner, but they kept their distance.

Tessa loved playing the part of submissive, and did it well.

But Matteo wasn't the Angelico brother Tessa wanted to submit to.

She glanced at the clock. If she moved quickly enough, she would have just enough time to stash the contents of her front seat behind the dumpster, and pray to God no one would find it. The rest would have to be explained away. She sighed as she stepped quickly out of *Cara's*. She'd done her very best to move *past* this shit, the sneaking, and the anxiety, the nerves and pressure.

When *would* she get her shit together for real?

Chapter 2

From somewhere beneath the mountain of papers on his desk, Tony's phone chirped and drew his attention away from the computer screen for the first time in hours. He shoved his chair back and rubbed the knot that had formed in his neck.

God, he hated spending time behind a desk when he could be out in the kitchen.

But things were looking good. Damn good. Income had been consistently high all summer and didn't appear to be slowing too much, even as the weather turned colder and tourist season ended. Costs were down, well, only *slightly*, but that was still a win. *Cara* looked to turn a profit again this quarter. And the mountain of debt he'd accumulated during last spring's renovation and unexpected kitchen repairs would finally, *finally* be paid off.

He typed out a quick email to Tess—*I read your report. Looks awesome. Keep doing what you're doing.*

And it really *was* her doing. He knew his control freak brothers would shake their heads at him for not keeping stricter control over every single detail of his business finances, but he'd opened his restaurant so he could *cook*, not crunch numbers. Profit and loss, cash flow reports, tracking capital expenses—all that shit gave him hives, and he was man enough to own the fact that he *sucked* at it.

No coincidence that ten months after he'd hired the lovely and talented Miss Damon as front end manager, they'd had their third profitable quarter. He didn't know exactly *how* she did it, and God knew he didn't want to. But she'd done it. She'd helped him take his dream, which had quickly turned into a nightmare of overdue bills and employment hassles, and make it into a thriving business.

His phone chirped again, and with a sigh he sifted through the papers until he found it.

And then quickly wished he hadn't.

Tony, I really need to talk to you. CALL ME.

Tony clicked the screen off and tossed the phone down on the desk as irritation pooled in the pit of his stomach. Another day, another annoying text message from Val, the ex-girlfriend who just wouldn't go away.

He scrubbed a hand over his forehead.

Part of him, a *big* part, wanted to call her and tell her *flat out* to get the fuck out of his life. Now that they were apart, he could see just how messed up things between them had been from the very beginning, and the whole thing disgusted him—her constant whining and demands, her superficial, materialistic insistence on looking the *best*, having the *best*, no matter the cost.

But an even larger part of him recognized his weak-assed passivity in allowing her to get her own way, his own role in the debacle, and he was able to rein in his temper. Yeah, at the time he'd thought that giving in was his way of supporting her, of showing that he cared, but now he could see that he'd been wrong. The relationship hadn't been healthy, not for either of them. And not for the people around them.

His mind helpfully dredged up an image of a shaking,

sobbing, humiliated Tess running out of the function room during his brother Dominic's rehearsal dinner last month. Val had accused Tony of being attracted to Tess, and accused Tess of trying to seduce Tony, on the basis of nothing more than a few shared looks and smiles. He sighed.

It sucked that it had come to that. It sucked that Tess had gotten hurt. But that moment had made him realize, far more effectively than the hundred lectures from his brothers or the red numbers on his bank balance, just how doomed his relationship with Val had been. Because his first thought, beyond shock and anger, had been, "Christ, don't I *wish* Tess had tried to seduce me!"

Followed quickly by, "Well, shit. Val's right. I *am* attracted to Tess."

So it was kind of hard to stay mad at Val, because in some ways she'd been the smartest one of all of them. She'd known that his heart hadn't been in the relationship long before Tony had figured that fact out for himself, and she'd called him out on an attraction to Tess that he hadn't wanted to acknowledge.

Of course, that didn't mean he wanted to talk to Val ever again, either.

He grabbed the phone and stared at it, debating if and how to reply, when a knock on the doorframe of his open office door had him glancing up…

And promptly swallowing his tongue.

Jesus.

Auburn hair had fallen from her clip to frame her pale, heart-shaped face. Those clear brown eyes that showed every emotion were undercut with pale lavender shadows that made her seem more fragile than he knew her to be. And that *dress*—that thin green *thing* that looked like it had been poured over her, hugging every curve, was tied in a cute little bow that just begged him to unwrap her like it was his birthday and she was his present. Just the sight of her had him growing hard and scooting his chair under the desk to hide it.

Most of the time, he was prepared to see her—his body on a low-level lockdown that enabled him to look at her and actually *converse* with her without stammering or springing an erection like a fucking teenager. But other times? S*hit*. Her beauty just stunned him.

"Hey," she said. "Ready to go?"

"Go?" He blinked, dazed.

She smiled. "To the *mechanic*?" She said each word slowly, teasing him. "To get your *car*?" She put her two hands out on an imaginary steering wheel and pretended to drive.

He shook his head to clear it. "Yeah. Yeah, sorry. I, uh… I was looking at the reports you sent and lost track of time," he explained.

"Ohh!" she said with a knowing wink, leaning one shoulder against the doorframe. "The numbers have all started to dance before your eyes, haven't they?"

Tony felt the corner of his mouth twitch. She knew him well.

"You should've waited and read the report right before bed," Tess continued, her eyes twinkling. "No tossing and turning. You'd be out like a light." She snapped her fingers in illustration.

Tony snorted and rolled his eyes. "I can think of better ways to relax before bed."

He didn't process the words as he spoke them, and it was too late to call them back. And damn, now he was watching her *and* thinking about all the many, many ways they could…

She cleared her throat, a tiny, nervous sound, and his cock twitched.

Gah! Down, boy. You're her boss, for God's sake, and her friend.

He took a deep breath and sailed on, as though he hadn't just been imagining her luscious body spread out on his sheets. "Uh, you know, like, uh… reading books. Watching old episodes of MacGyver on Netflix. That kind of thing."

She nodded slowly. "I like reading," she said. And was he imagining that her voice was husky?

Stop. It.

"Um, awesome job, by the way," he told her, lifting a hand toward the computer monitor where the monthly profit and loss was still displayed. "Honest to God, Tess, I don't know what I'd do without you."

"Oh!" she stammered shyly, maybe surprised by his change of topic. "It's, you know, no big deal."

"It is to me."

Her face flushed pink and she lowered her eyes in a way that only made the problem he was hiding under the desk even worse. *Damn it.* He had no fucking control where this girl was concerned.

"Hey, could you give me a minute? Almost ready to go. I've just got to, uh… you know," he said lamely, not sure how to finish the sentence.

Adjust myself? Think about Mrs. Cuddy, the pinch-faced old battleax who screamed at me incessantly through three years of JV soccer? Recite the multiplication table? Do anything but stare at you.

"Finish your text?" she supplied, glancing down at the phone in his hands.

"*Yes.* Exactly. Send a text," he agreed, relieved.

"Is it to Matt?" she asked, taking a step forward and looking down at his phone. "Because I wanted to ask him—"

He recognized the exact moment she read Val's name upside down.

She straightened, she flushed, and for just one second, her eyes flashed with a mixture of confusion and hurt that seared his gut.

She turned away. "I'll just wait in the car," she said stiffly.

He closed his eyes briefly as she walked out.

He wanted to explain, but what the hell would he say? Besides, obviously his dick needed a reality check. Tessa Damon wasn't for the likes of him. Because among her other revelations at the rehearsal dinner, Val had told him and everyone else in earshot that Tess was a *submissive*. One who liked to hang out at The Club where Matteo worked and let herself be bossed around, *dominated*, by men.

It was still hard to wrap his mind around the concept. Tess, the woman who took no shit from even the surliest of the line cooks and had actually tossed a glass of red wine in Val's face, enjoyed that kind of thing? But the look on Matteo's face had confirmed it.

She wanted a guy like his brothers—a testosterone-oozing badass type, the kind who always needed to be in charge and get his way, the kind who had no problem spanking a woman's ass as long as she allowed it.

Dom and Matteo were good men, the *best*. They adored Heidi and Hillary. And Tony didn't give a shit what they did behind closed doors.

But he wasn't like them. The very idea of hurting Tess, of *anyone* hurting Tess, set his protective instincts aflame and had him gripping the edge of the desk.

It's none of your fucking business, he reminded himself. *She's not yours.*

And the helpless anger that overcame him with that thought cooled his ardor in a way that all the multiplication tables in the world couldn't.

He flung himself back from the desk, shoved his cell in his pocket, grabbed his keys and walked out, closing the office door behind him with a vicious slam.

"You're gonna have to direct me," Tess said softly as she steered her little blue car down Storrow Drive.

They were practically the first words they'd spoken to one

another since he'd gotten in the car, and they did nothing to calm his temper.

Neither did the way her dress rode up her legs each time she shifted in her seat, exposing a row of golden brown freckles on her creamy white thigh. Nor the way she modestly pulled the dress back down at regular intervals, hiding those intriguing freckles from his view.

"Take the Kenmore exit," he said brusquely. "It's coming up."

She put on her blinker and moved to the right hand lane without comment.

He sighed.

None of this was her fault—not his irritation at Val, nor his inability to be an alpha superhero like his brothers, nor his lack of control over his damn cock. She was doing him a favor. And he was being an asshole.

"Sorry," he said with a sigh.

She glanced over at him, then back at the road, and he noticed again that her eyes looked tired. Worn out. She exhaled slowly and shrugged. "It's fine."

"It's *not*," he disagreed. After a moment, he continued, "Val's texted me a few times. I haven't responded. I don't want to give in to her, and I don't want to talk to her. I think I'm going to have to block her."

Traffic in the right-hand lane all but stopped and he realized belatedly that there was a Sox game tonight. They'd be crawling all the way to the mechanic.

Wasn't *that* the fucking cherry on the sundae?

His irritation ratcheted up another notch and he fumed silently.

Tess darted another glance at him.

"I think you *should* talk to her," she said.

Tony grunted, a sound of disagreement.

"Seriously. What if she's trying to tell you that she's pregnant?"

God, now *there* was a thought to make his balls shrivel in his pants.

"I used a condom every time and we haven't had sex in four months," he said flatly. "It'd be a little late now."

"Gahhhh! Jeez, Tony! TMI, much?" she said, as if disgusted, but he just shrugged. It was the truth, and anyway, she was the one who'd brought it up.

"Oookay, well... what if she found a million dollars in loose change under the seat cushion and she wants to share it with you?"

Tony snorted, though he felt his bad mood start to lighten with her attempt at humor. "She can keep it."

Tess snickered. "Wow! Big talk! What's the weather like where *you* live, Mr. Moneybags?"

He rolled his eyes. "I'm just saying, I don't want to spend another minute with her, even for half a million dollars."

"Idealistic. I respect that," Tess mused, auburn strands dancing around her face as she nodded. "But let *me* just say that for half a million dollars, I'd tie you up, toss you in the back seat, and *deliver* you to her," she teased.

Against all odds, Tony found himself fighting a smile. "That's how much your loyalty is worth? Only half a mill?" He clutched his chest in mock disappointment. "I'm heartbroken, Damon. I'm worth ten mill at least."

An expression Tony couldn't decipher crossed her beautiful face before she smiled halfheartedly.

"If it makes you feel better, I'd deliver Matt for half that," she offered.

Somehow, absurdly, it *did*. Plus, the idea of Matteo all trussed up and dumped on Val's doorstep...

"I might have to take you up on that," he told her. And then she glanced up at him quickly, their eyes met, and they both burst out laughing.

"To be honest, though," he said, glancing in the back seat of her car for the first time, "I don't think there's room for either one of us back there."

Two clear plastic totes full of clothes were stacked on the seat behind Tess, and a cardboard box of books had been squished onto the floor beneath. Craning his head, he saw more totes and boxes piled behind him, along with a small bag of food and a bundled up sleeping bag stowed on the floor.

He vaguely remembered overhearing her talk to Hillary the other day.

He smacked his forehead with his palm.

"Ah, shit! You're moving aren't you? I completely forgot!"

She shrugged like it wasn't a big deal.

"Why didn't you schedule some time off?" he demanded. "And I would have helped!"

"Oh, look!" she interrupted. "Traffic's moving. Which street do I take?"

"Bear right, down Park Drive, then your second right onto Queensborough."

She looked at him with something like suspicion in her wide eyes. "I thought you said we were going to a mechanic!" she said.

He raised an eyebrow. "Well, *yeah*. My friend Nick is a mechanic, and he rents a couple parking spots behind a building where he does light repairs—oil changes, belts, tires, that kind of shit. The stuff you don't need a lift to… Wait, why would you think we *weren't* going to the mechanic?" he asked.

Tess took a deep breath. "I'm just familiar with this street, that's all. And I didn't remember a garage."

Tony stared at her in confusion as she focused all of her attention on the road, deliberately avoiding his gaze.

"Tess?" His voice was low and serious.

She sighed. "The Club is on this street," she said reluctantly.

He sat back in his seat. "Oh. Yeah, I guess I knew it was in this neighborhood somewhere. But why in the world would you think I'd want to go *there?*" he asked.

Like the place was a leper colony. Could you be *more* of an asshole, Tony?

Her face flushed. "I... I didn't. I guess I *wasn't* thinking. Sorry."

He scrubbed his hand over his head in frustration. Would there ever be a time when he wasn't putting his foot in his mouth with this girl?

"No, I'm sorry. Again. And I have nothing against the place, I've just never been there, that's all. Which clearly puts me in the minority among my friends and family," he said, only partly joking. "Some of my favorite people hang out there."

She looked at him shyly. "But you never, uh..."

Her hand fluttered through the air, as though she was too embarrassed to finish the thought. Despite the seriousness of the topic, she was so freakin' adorable he found himself grinning again.

"Never, uh, *what?*" he asked.

She shot him a sideways glare.

"Spit it out, Damon," he drawled.

She huffed and rolled her eyes. "Fine. You've never been interested in kink?"

He shook his head. "Nope. I'm not into the whole pain-thing, giving or receiving."

"Well, right," she said slowly. "A lot of people aren't into pain." He noticed that she didn't say whether *she* was into it. "I meant the other stuff."

He looked over at her skeptically. "You mean giving rules, that kind of stuff? It's kinda all the same thing, isn't it? Just an excuse for the pain."

She maneuvered the car into an empty spot on the side of

the street and turned to look at him fully. "Are you kidding?" Her eyes held his and he frowned.

"Kidding about what?"

"There's a big difference between dominance and submission as opposed to sadism and masochism," she said. "And it's not all physical. There's an emotional connection, a level of trust between a submissive and her partner. That's the best part."

The autumn sun was low in the sky, turning her brown eyes to a glowing topaz. He could smell her perfume—something musky and citrusy. There was no place in the world he would rather be at this moment.

There was no topic he was less excited to discuss.

He shrugged and blew out a breath. "To be honest, I haven't really researched all the subtleties," he told her, wincing at the defensiveness in his own voice.

She shook her head, incredulous. "It's not really a *subtle* difference, Tony. It's like the difference between... I dunno... Monster trucks and televised golf."

"God, the things you say, Damon!" He grinned appreciatively. Who else on earth could make him laugh about this shit, while looking like a wet dream come to life and staring at him like he was a moron? Answer: not one single other person. And maybe that was why his voice was soft and remorseful as he told her, "You may be right, but I'm not really into either one."

Her head went back and she sucked in a breath. Then she nodded slowly and straightened in her seat, tugging her skirt down her thighs once again.

He grabbed the door handle and pushed the door open.

"See you back at the restaurant?" he asked.

"You know it, boss!" she chirped. She tossed him a smile, but her eyes didn't meet his. And once again, he noticed how tired she looked. Was she getting enough rest?

Damn it.

"Hey, thanks for the lift," he said.

He reached over and put his hand on her shoulder, and she turned to look at him.

Her eyes softened. "Anytime, Tony."

He smiled. "And thanks for the advice."

She rolled her eyes. "Yeah, right. Are you actually going to call her?" she demanded, smiling.

"What? And deprive you of your ransom payment when you deliver me? Tessa, I wouldn't dream of it."

She grinned at him fully, a wide white smile that made his heart stop.

She's not yours, idiot.

He got out of the car, stood on the curb, slammed the door shut behind him, and raised his hand in a wave. But as she pulled out into the road and he watched her drive away, he still felt like he'd lost something very precious.

"Night, Tony!" Nicole called, raising her hand in a salute.

Tony glanced up from the rack of veal he'd been prepping for tomorrow, his hands coated in garlic, olive oil, and rosemary, and he frowned.

"Everything cleaned up already?" he asked, glancing at the clock. It felt like only a few minutes since he'd said goodnight to Max and Virginia Martin, and congratulated them one final time on their silver wedding anniversary.

Nicole shook her head. "Nah, not quite. They're almost done, though, so Tess said I could bounce. There's a band at The Cask and my friends are saving me a seat," she said, as though this should explain everything.

Tony bit his tongue and forced himself to nod. If Nicole went home early, that left Tess and Hillary to stay even later cleaning up from the party—boxing up the food to be delivered to the homeless shelter tomorrow, breaking down the tables, vacuuming, even washing the dishes, since the kitchen staff had all gone home after the main restaurant closed at 11. And he knew that was Tess's call as manager, but *damn*… Tess's eyes had looked so tired earlier today.

"Later!" Nicole chirped as she collected her things and scooted out the fire door to the alley.

"Hey, you need me to walk you to your car?" Tony yelled belatedly.

"I'm good!" she called back.

Tony sighed and wrapped a piece of cling wrap around the meat. Tomorrow it would be turned into *Cara's* signature Arrosto de Vitello, a recipe he'd created and honed to perfection over the years, but Tony wouldn't be there. Tomorrow, he had the whole day off for the first time in weeks. He couldn't fucking wait. He planned to binge-watch the latest season of *House of Cards*, maybe take in some fall foliage…

Ah, whom was he kidding? He'd spend the day working up some new recipes in his home kitchen, because he was a glutton for punishment like that.

He put the meat in the fridge, washed and sanitized his workstation, and went to volunteer for the cleanup crew.

When he pushed open the swinging door to the function room, he saw that all of the dishes had been cleared, and Hillary was busy collecting table linens while Tess mechanically boxed up leftovers from the buffet table. Without a word, he began folding chairs and stacking them on the large dolly they used to transport them to the stockroom.

Hillary gave him a grateful smile. "Thanks, boss man!"

Tony grunted. "No problem, Tink."

Tess looked over from the buffet table. "You shouldn't be doing that!" she scolded sharply.

Tony raised his eyebrows and glanced at her, not saying a word. She flushed and looked away.

"I just meant it's not your job and I know you have more important things to do," she said in a small voice.

"Uh huh," Tony said, equally amused and annoyed by her burst of temper. "Well, it just so happens that all of my very important things are done for today. So unless the President calls and needs my advice, I can fold a damn chair in my own restaurant."

Tess flushed an even deeper red as Hillary snickered.

"Does the President often call for your help?" Hillary teased. "Like, 'I have a manicotti emergency, Tony, and you're the only one who can help!' "

Tony folded his arms over his chest and adopted his most serious expression. "Can't answer that, Hillary. For your own safety. You know I'm not allowed to talk about matters of national security."

Hillary laughed out loud at his ridiculousness, but it was Tess's barely-audible chuckle that sent a wave of euphoria through him. He was unreasonably proud of himself for breaking her out of her shitty mood, at least temporarily. If he were with her, he'd make a point to...

Irrelevant, man.

"Actually, I find folding chairs very Zen," he told Hillary in the same mock-serious voice. "It's got this rhythm that helps clear my mind. Fold, turn, stack, repeat..."

"The path to enlightenment lies in folding chairs?" Tess asked skeptically.

"Indeed, grasshopper," Tony told her, smirking. "I have much to teach you."

Tess huffed out a laugh again. *Win.*

"Oh, hey! Speaking of moving chairs!" Hillary interjected. "What's the plan for this weekend, Tess? Do you want Matt and me over on Saturday or just Sunday? Oh, and maybe Mr. Enlightenment over here can come flex his muscles for you, too," she said, giving Tony a wink.

Tony nodded.

Tess swung around to face Hillary, wide-eyed. "What? Were you supposed to come over Sunday?"

Hillary cocked her head to the side. "Yes, silly! To help you move to your new place! Remember?"

Tess shook her head wildly.

Hillary scrunched up her face. "We were in your office, right after I told you Matt knows your new landlord from *Inked*," she explained, referring to the tattoo parlor where Matteo rented a chair. "I said he put in a good word for you, and you said that was great and now all you needed was someone to help you move, and I volunteered! I put it right on my calendar!" She pulled out her phone for confirmation.

"I... oh, gosh. Oh, Hill, I'm so sorry!" Tess said, covering her eyes with her palm. "I completely forgot to tell you! It, um... things, uh... fell through. I'm not moving after all!"

Tony turned to frown at her. If she wasn't moving, what was all that crap in her backseat?

Hillary must've been suspicious, too, because she stopped and turned to look at Tess fully.

"But you said your mom was planning to let a friend crash in your old room."

Tess nodded, darting a nervous glance between Tony and Hillary. "Uh... that's true. Yup."

Hillary planted her hands on her hips and looked at Tess expectantly. "So you *are* moving."

Tess flushed. "I mean, I'm moving *out*, yes, just not moving *in* to the place I was planning to rent."

Okay, yeah, this was officially strange. Alarm bells began to go off in Tony's head.

"Where *are* you moving to, then?" he asked.

Tess flushed. "Not sure yet. A couple of people have offered to let me stay with them," she said softly. "Until I can find a new place."

Tony appraised her and replayed her words in his mind. Tess was always so careful not to tell lies, but that didn't mean she always told the whole truth. Just because someone had offered, that didn't mean she'd accepted.

"So, which friend are you staying with?" Tony asked, point-blank.

Tess froze. "Well, I haven't fully decided yet," she said vaguely. "Eva, maybe."

"Eva, your friend from high school with the crazy boyfriend and the one-bedroom apartment? I didn't know you guys hung out anymore," Hillary said. "That sucks, Tess! If only we hadn't rented Heidi's old place out!"

Tess shrugged and gave a brittle smile. "Oh, well! Things always work out for the best!"

Hillary grimaced. "But I know how excited you were to not have a roommate," she said, her voice gentle and sympathetic. "It sucks to have to couch surf when you really wanted your *own* space."

Tess shrugged again. "It's not ideal," she said brightly. "But I really don't mind staying with a friend! We'll stay out of each other's way, and it'll be fine. It's only temporary!"

Tony wondered if she knew how desperate she sounded.

Hillary looked like she would say more, but a buzz from the rear door cut her off.

"Oh, Matt must be here to pick me up!" she said, and her eyes filled with excitement, as though it had been days rather than hours since she'd seen her man. She walked quickly towards the kitchen, taking a moment to comb her fingers through her wavy blonde hair and straighten her shirt.

Tony glanced at Tess and they exchanged a smirk.

Young love. So cute.

"So… Tell me more about this moving situation," Tony said, folding his arms over his chest. Tess's shoulders stiffened and she drew a deep breath.

"Tony, I appreciate your concern. You're a good guy. A good friend. But I'm fine, and I…"

"You know, I am so glad you said that," Tony interjected, as an idea sprang to his mind.

Tess scowled. "Said what? That I'm fine?"

"No," Tony mused. "Well, I mean, *yes*, that too, of course. But I'm really glad you said that we're *friends*. Because we are, Tess. Good friends."

Tess looked at him like he was crazy. A voice in the back of his head suggested that maybe she was right, but the facts had all clicked into place in his mind, finally, so he ignored that voice.

"And Tess, friends don't let friends do stupid shit," he told her. "Shit that's dangerous or unhealthy, shit that could get them hurt."

She licked her lips nervously, and his cock took that opportunity to remind him that this was *Tess* and she was just as irresistible as she'd been a few hours ago.

Damn it.

"What are you talking about?" she demanded.

"I'm talking about you having all of your possessions and your sleeping bag in your car, Miss Damon. I'm talking about you not having a place to stay."

Her eyes widened and her face blanched.

"I… you… I have a place to stay!" she stammered.

"Hmmm. With your friend and her boyfriend? On her couch? Maybe," Tony agreed. Another thought occurred to him, and he went with it. "Or maybe you haven't even told her you needed a place to stay."

Tess's face went from pale to flushed and Tony shook his head.

"*Fuck. Me.* I'm right, aren't I?" he demanded, a sudden and ferocious anger churning in his stomach. "Jesus Christ, Tessa! Why didn't you tell me? Why didn't you tell *anyone*? I can think of a dozen people who would have helped you out—maybe more!

What the *hell* were you thinking? If you need a place to stay, you…"

"I don't *need* help!" she whispered angrily. "And I don't *want* help from you or from anyone else. I can take care of *myself*, Anthony Angelico."

Despite the fact that his temper had reached stratospheric levels, he felt the impact of those two words, his full name coming from those perfect lips, zing up his spine. *God help him.*

"Who made the money in my checking account?" she hissed, stepping toward him with one accusing finger pointed at his chest. "Who pays my bills? Who takes care of my sister when my fucking mother screws her over again? *I. Do.* Understand?"

Oh, he understood, all right. Way more than she probably realized. His chest burned at the pain in her voice.

The thought flitted across his mind, as he stood there watching her trembling in desperate fury, her brown eyes glowing gold like she was some kind of avenging angel, that Tessa Damon must be the worst fucking submissive at The Club. There wasn't a weak bone in this woman's body.

But if there was one thing that being the youngest Angelico brother had taught him, it was persistence. He was never the strongest or the fastest, but he was damn well able to hang on the longest. And like Tessa, he knew how to employ selective truth telling when the situation required.

He tamped down his anger and grabbed for control with both hands.

"I wasn't offering you a handout, Damon," he told her, holding his hands up, palms out, and smiling. "Jeez! Don't get your panties in a twist."

Her eyes narrowed in confusion. "You *just* said…"

"I just said I had a place to stay if you wanted one," he told her, widening his eyes innocently. "I was thinking we could help *each other* out. See, I live in a two-bedroom apartment, and my lease isn't up until April." This was truth, and she knew it. She blinked.

Encouraged, he continued, "But you know, things have been kinda tight, what with the loans for the restaurant renovation and stuff." Not precisely true, since the "tightness" was in his business financials—he still drew a decent salary. But he sighed in frustration, and that seemed to sell her. Her eyes were lit with sympathy.

"I could take a roommate," he said pensively, mentally adding *when pigs fly*. "But I hate the idea of living with a stranger." Absolute truth. "So, you see, it was kind of selfish of you to not share your situation with me, because this could work out perfectly for both of us," he concluded. "You could live with me. As my roommate. Temporarily."

"Live with you?" she said slowly. She blinked several more times, and the tension in his belly eased a fraction. "If I agreed, it would help you out?"

He'd known that would be the clincher. Was it manipulative? Maybe. But also wasn't a lie. Hell, yes, she'd be helping him out by moving in. For one thing, he wouldn't have to carry her bodily into his apartment and tie her down, which is exactly what he'd do if she didn't agree. Damned if she was spending another night in a fucking parking lot.

"What's the rent?" she asked. Oh, yes. She was thinking about it.

"Uh…" The truth was, he lived in a fairly expensive apartment with a partial view of the Charles River. He knew how much she made, and knew that splitting his rent was way more than she could afford. He scrambled for a number that wasn't suspiciously low or disappointingly high. "Eight hundred a month would be fair."

"Shut up," she said, shaking her head. "You live in Gallery Towers, Tony."

He winced. "Yeah, but the second bedroom is *way* smaller. Plus, you don't get an en-suite."

She pursed her lips and thought about it. Then shook her head. "I just don't know."

She left him no choice but to play his final card.

"Gotta be honest, Tess. I'm not letting my manager sleep in her car anymore. You ran into a situation with your apartment falling through? That sucks. But shit happens to everyone. And I get you're all independent and whatever, but deciding to sleep in your car 'cause you're too proud to admit that you need an assist? It's stupid. And I'm not sure I want to employ someone who's that fucking dumb. If you don't move in with me, or find a decent situation immediately, meaning *tonight*, you're fired."

She seemed to be struck dumb for a moment. Then her eyes widened, her jaw dropped, and she let out a little squawk that could have been a sound of hurt or outrage, or the precursor to lava erupting from her eyes…

Or, apparently, laughter.

He should have known to expect the unexpected when it came to Tessa.

The crazy woman burst into giggles. She covered her mouth with her hand, but couldn't repress it.

"Oh, my God. You… are… amazing!" she told him.

And then she *really* shocked him.

She threw her arms around his neck and planted the tiniest kiss on his cheek.

It only lasted a moment, so fast he barely had time to put his arms around her and catch the faintest hint of her perfume before she rocked back on her feet, but it was enough to wake up his cock.

Damn nuisance.

"I don't understand what's funny," he told her, setting his jaw and folding his arms across his chest. "I'm dead serious."

She smiled. "I know you are, and I know you'd follow through. But for you to take that step, you must be really, *really* worried about me, and that's sweet. I happen to know you get a migraine just looking at the daily intake reports." She shook her head, still smiling. "So, fine, you win. I'll move in with you. As your roommate. Just temporarily. Like, *very* temporarily. And only because it will help you out, too."

Hmmm. Well, they could work out the details later.

"And because I'm *sweet*?" Tony asked.

She frowned a little and looked away. "Er… something like that. And because, well… it *is* dangerous and silly," she conceded. "If my sister Nora was doing it, I…"

"Stupid," he corrected her. "Dangerous and *stupid*."

She scowled and inhaled sharply like she would argue, but he raised one eyebrow and looked at her sternly, and she seemed to deflate.

"Yeah," she finally agreed in a low voice. "That too."

He held his position for another minute waiting for her to argue again—Lord knew, the woman always had some snappy comeback to make. But this time she didn't.

Huh.

Instead, she went back to the buffet table and finished boxing up the food. He noticed that her step seemed lighter, somehow.

"All right, kids!" Matteo said, standing in the doorway and clapping his hands together once. "Let's get this show on the road. My woman and I are eager to get home!"

Tess snorted and glanced over her shoulder at Tony, rolling her eyes at Matt's eagerness. Tony smirked back.

But for once, he and his brother were in absolute agreement. Tonight, Tony couldn't wait to get home, either.

Chapter 3

"See, and this is why I can't stand these shows," Tessa said, gesturing to the television as she shook her head, her lips pursed. "*Clearly*, she isn't a zombie! First, you can see her chest rising up and down, and anyone who knows anything about zombies knows that they're *dead*. Why would her chest be rising up and down like that?"

Tony sighed with practiced patience, leaning forward from his seat on the sofa. He rested his arms on his knees, his fingertips coming together as he leaned forward. "See, you're just perpetuating a zombie myth," he said with a sad shake of his head. "Yes, zombies are dead. But a small part of their heart, lungs, and brain still work. This is what makes them able to function! Plus, this zombie chick probably was used to breathing for, what, twenty or twenty-five years? You think just because you're dead you forget how to breathe?"

"You mean fifteen years. She can't be a day over fifteen."

"No way!"

"Yes way! And furthermore, did you see how she stopped and showed compassion to the puppy trapped in the car on the bridge? Zombies do not show their compassion. That's the way zombies roll. Dead. Not conscious. *No compassion or emotional reaction.*"

Tony nodded. Now they were getting somewhere.

"And she cut herself and was bleeding. Ridiculous! Even the most basic second-grader knows zombies do not bleed! Hello?"

"You'd let a second-grader watch this zombie movie? Are you crazy?"

"I didn't say that! But sure, second-graders play zombies on playgrounds."

"We played cops and robbers, not *zombies*. You played zombies?"

She shrugged. "Maybe. But listen! Final fact that proves the creators of this movie knew nothing about zombies."

He nodded.

"Have you noticed how nicely manicured her nails were? She's dead! Dead people do not have nicely manicured nails."

Tony looked soberly at her, with admiration. "Impressive. It's like you did a thesis on zombies in college or something."

Tessa felt her cheeks flush slightly, as she cleared her throat. "I, um, may have."

He grinned, and her cheeks flushed deeper, for an entirely different reason.

"My question is," Tony continued, "what kind of a moron goes out to their car in the middle of the night, alone? Who parks their car in a dark alley to begin with? That girl deserved to be zombified."

"No one deserves to be zombified! What a horrible thing to say!"

"There are definitely people who deserve to be zombified. For example—people who let second-graders watch zombie movies. And women who park their cars in dark alleys and go out to them alone in the middle of the night."

"No one deserves zombification," she insisted with a serious shake of her head. He nodded soberly.

"You know, you're right. My brothers would say what she needs is a good spanking."

Her cheeks flamed, and she squeezed her eyes shut. She wasn't sure if she could trust herself to speak for a moment, as she fought to get control of her emotions, mostly flaming hot cheeks and a pounding heart because of the fact he'd just said someone needed *a good spanking*. Thankfully, the doorbell rang and she sprang to her feet.

"Don't even think about it, Tess," Tony said warningly. "I said no!"

Like he was gonna do anything about it? Ha! She'd been moved into his apartment as his roommate for a solid three weeks, and they'd gotten takeout precisely three times. He'd insisted on paying every time and hadn't taken a penny from her, but this time would be different.

"Back off, Angelico," she said, hustling to the door ahead of him. What he didn't know is that she already had the cash tucked into her pocket, exact change plus tip, and she'd planned her move. Distract him, open the door, shove cash in the delivery person's hand.

"Oh, Tony, what's that on the balcony? Did another one of the baby birds get injured? Look!" She pointed a finger, and he actually fell for it, turning to the sliding glass door of the balcony. A mama bird had built a nest right outside the balcony door, conveniently tucked into the wrought iron railing, and some creature had gotten to one of the birds a few days prior. To Tessa's immense pleasure, Tony had actually brought the bird inside, gingerly carrying it in his Red Sox cap and calling his friend who worked at a nearby animal shelter. It was the cutest thing Tess had ever seen. She watched gleefully now as he fell for it, turning to the balcony. She sprinted to the door. The tall, gangly teen with a shock of red hair and glasses perched on his nose blinked as she yanked open the door, smiled her thanks, shoved the cash in his hand, and grabbed the box.

"Thanks so much. Have a good night!" she said, and the door was shut in the boy's face before Tony had recovered from the fake out.

Still facing the door, she held the box in her hand, not quite ready to face Tony. She'd planned the whole thing before the food got there. What she hadn't planned was how to deal with him after she'd fooled him. Slowly, she turned around, and she knew the look on her face was sheepish.

"So, you say this is the best pizza in Boston, huh?" she said quickly. "Why don't you get us some plates, and I'll get us some drinks. Phew, am I hungry. So famished, I actually feel a little faint! Can you..."

Her voice trailed off as her fast-talking move wasn't doing a damn thing. Tony was standing in front of her, and was it her imagination or did she shrink or something? She didn't remember him being this much taller than she was. Damn it, wearing heels to work had decided advantages. Those eyes! Oh, God, his eyes were narrowed on her in a teasing, but still sexy-stern way that made her heart flutter in her chest.

"Hungry," she stuttered helplessly. "Faint... with hunger."

He stalked closer to her, and the only thing between him and her was a flimsy cardboard box, which he removed with one firm pull. She squealed.

He placed the box on the dining room table, then continued to prowl closer to her. She backpedaled until he had her pinned against the door, and her hands went flat out behind her, splayed on the cool frame of the door.

"Are you really faint with hunger? Or is that another one of your *fibs*, Miss Damon?"

Oh, she was definitely faint, but she was sure it wasn't from hunger. Her knees trembled and she was so turned on, it was mortifying. She swallowed, an impossible giggle bubbling up.

"Fib? Who says fib?" she snorted. Gosh, his word choices were so adorable sometimes.

He raised his eyebrows incredulously. "First, you fake me out so you can have your way even though I insisted I was paying, you told a *fib*, and now you'll insult me?"

He was so close she could see the flecks in the depths of his hazel eyes.

"It's just cute," she said helplessly, immediately wishing she could take it back. His eyes softened a little.

"I'll modify my earlier statement," he said, and he was so close, with his arms crossed on his chest, she could feel his heat, smell the faint sporty smell of the body wash he had in the shower that she surreptitiously lifted the lid on and sniffed every time she took a shower herself. "People who let second-graders watch zombie movies. Women who go to dark alleys alone in the middle of the night. And people who tell fibs to fake someone out so the guy can't pay for the food he's gonna eat most of anyway. *Those* are the people who need be *spanked*."

It was a sheer act of will that kept her standing.

"Is that right?" she whispered, and her voice was husky. But it was just a threat. She knew he wasn't into the whole spanking chicks thing. But just the idea of it... all he had to do was take her by the hand, and lead her to one of the chairs that flanked the dining room table. Oh, God. With one firm pull, he'd have her belly-down over his lap. Oh, *God*. And he'd said before that his *brothers* would say she needed a spanking. Now he was using the words "need to be spanked," all on his own, not referring to the twitchy palms of Matteo or Dom, but his own large, capable, masculine—

Her phone rang.

"I need to get that," she whispered. "I've got to take that call." It was Nora's ring.

He stepped back quickly and nodded. The moment was lost, but she'd replay *that* one a good many times, she reflected, as she trotted over to the end table to retrieve her phone.

"Hey," she said cheerfully, steeling herself to whatever

would come. Nora called her daily, and lately, most of the calls were decent. She spent more of her time out of the house, and was rarely home when their mother and her obnoxious boyfriends were. But there were a few times Tessa had answered the phone, only to hear Nora's irate voice, or, worse, her sobs.

Though she had her back to Tony, she could feel his eyes on her as she spoke with Nora.

"What's up, hon?"

Tessa had been completely honest with her sister, and hadn't held anything back when she moved in with Tony. The only thing she'd hidden from Nora was the fact that she hadn't had a place to live and had stayed in her car for a time, because she knew Nora would feel horrible.

"Quick question, Tess. My English class has a study group meeting at the library in five. But… well, I was wondering. Do you know anywhere I can get a job? I am *not* asking you for money. You've helped me so much. But I want my *own* money, something I can use to buy myself clothes, or go to a movie with my friends or something. Can you just think about it and let me know?"

"Sure thing, baby," Tess said, as she took the plate of pizza and salad Tony gave her. He'd even drizzled salad dressing on it for her. She winked at him to thank him, and he grinned at her. She eyed his own plate with four pieces of pizza and not a trace of lettuce on it, and shook her head.

"Okay, thanks! Talk to you later?"

"Later. Love you." Tony's eyes flew to hers and he froze, pizza halfway to his mouth. She put the phone down and looked at him strangely.

"You okay?" She pulled out a chair, momentarily dazzled by the fantasy she'd played out of him pulling out the chair himself, and sat down. He pushed a glass of water over to her.

"Thanks," she said, still completely unaccustomed to how

chivalrous he was to her. She'd never been with a guy who did things like open the door for her, or hand her a plate of food.

It felt nice.

"Who was that?" he said, and his voice had a bit of an edge. Weird.

"Nora."

He knew about Nora and Eva, but that was about it.

"Everything cool?" He'd polished off two pieces to her one, and was picking up his third.

"Do you even *chew* your food?" she asked, shaking her head. "You Angelico brothers must've eaten your mama out of house and home."

"Course we did," he said around a mouthful of pizza. "You work up a big appetite, watching zombie movies. All those brains."

"Ewww!"

He snorted, as he ate half of the slice of pizza in one large gulp.

"Impressive," she murmured, with a grimace. "So, Nora's looking for work. I wonder if she can get a job sacking groceries at Stop and Shop or something. Or maybe they're hiring down at Lowe's, and she can get a job working the fall garden center. I'll have to ask around."

"Ask around?" he said, as he polished off the third slice. "Why don't you have her come work for us? She can bus. God, we need it. Nicole's been unreliable lately, and business is really picking up. Think she'd be interested in clearing tables and stuff? And we'd only need her for after school hours anyway. I'll pay her more than any of those other places would pay, too."

He was offering her baby sister a job? A lump rose to her throat, and her appetite fled. She swallowed. Nora would work with *her*, where she could watch over her, and see her on a regular basis, and know that Nora was working for a boss who would treat her well.

"That'd be great," she said. Her eyes watered and her nose stung. She swallowed a sip from her water and composed herself. "I'll call her tonight. She's at a study group now."

Tony reached for a fourth slice of pizza.

"Awesome," he said. "That'd be one less thing for me to worry about."

"Are you gonna touch any of this salad? God, you could feed a small army of rabbits with this thing."

He snorted. "And that's supposed to make me want to eat it?"

She giggled. "Guess not."

They ate in silence for a bit, but it wasn't awkward. Tess was comfortable around Tony. She'd worried at first that she wouldn't be able to relax around him, but it had turned out that wasn't a problem at all. He made her feel at ease. She felt like she could be herself around him. For the first time in her life, she was in a place she could return to at the end of a long day, and not have to worry about what would be waiting for her. A place where she could be at peace. And there was Tony.

His phone buzzed and he glanced at it casually.

"Val?" The minute the word left her mouth, she wished she could take it back. His eyes widened in surprise, and then shuttered. His jaw clenched, and he sat back in his chair.

"Not Val. You know I'm not with Val anymore."

And *why* did he feel the need to tell her that? She shrugged as nonchalantly as possible, which was probably way too forced and obvious.

"Sure. I know. But with the amount of texts she sends, it's like *way* over the friend zone, much less the ex-girlfriend zone."

Omg. Tess! Shut UP!

Why couldn't she stop talking? And why was she having this conversation? She took an enormous bite of her pizza, in the hopes that stuffing food in her mouth would stop the ridiculous flow of very unhelpful conversation.

"It's Matt. Headed into The Club. Wanted to ask me about

some event his friend wants to do at one point." He paused. "What kind of event would those people want to do?"

Those people? She looked down at the rest of the pizza she'd suddenly lost her appetite for.

"Those people are *my* people," she said quietly. She hadn't been to The Club in a while, but was planning on going the following evening. "They're normal people. At least *most* of them. I mean not *everyone* dresses in latex and leather. If they want an event at *Cara*, we should do it."

"Would your ex be there?"

Her eyes flew to his. "My ex?"

He shrugged, polishing off his pizza. "Matt said you go to The Club because an ex got you in. Just wondered if he still went."

"He's not there anymore, no," she said. Louie had moved to the West Coast years ago, and she'd lost touch with him.

Tony leaned back in his chair, and she couldn't help but notice how large his arms and hands were. It was one thing she loved about him. Other girls would fantasize about being kissed, or more, and sure, Tess let her mind wander in less-than-wholesome places a time or two herself, but what would it feel like to crawl into his lap? To feel his arms around her and snuggle her head on his chest? He was so big and strong, and sweet. Her fantasy, in which she ended up belly down over his lap and he paddled her soundly, sometimes ended not with hot and heavy sex, but being held on his lap after a spanking, while he kissed her tears away.

"So... do you um, wear the leather and latex?" he asked as he got to his feet. "You want a beer?"

Tessa snorted. "No thanks. I'm not into latex, but I don't exactly wear turtlenecks and full length skirts to The Club." She had a good variety of outfits she'd picked up, some at the consignment shop in town, and some that girls from The Club had gotten for her.

He mumbled something under his breath, but she didn't catch it. Then he spoke louder, over his shoulder.

"And, uh, when might be the next time you're going to The Club?"

Was he asking because he didn't want her to go? Or did he want to see her in full-on Club attire? She'd always changed at The Club when she was leaving from *Cara*.

"Why?" she asked with a teasing grin. "You want to make sure my outfit is appropriate? Or do you want to go with me?"

He sobered, and she wanted to take the words back. She *had* to learn to think before she spoke. Without conscious thought, her hands flexed on her thighs, where her scars were. In high school, when she was down on herself for saying something stupid, or for losing her temper, her go-to had been to harm herself.

He lifted the bottle to his lips and shook his head. "I don't think so," he said. "Not my thing."

"Yeah," she said, swallowing a sigh. "That's what I thought."

Even if he *was* interested in her, though, could she give up what she loved? She craved what she found at The Club, being accepted by people just like her, the edgy group of people who loved deeply and did not judge. She soared when she submitted to a spanking, the hormonal release and erotic charge like drugs. Discovering her attraction to submission had been so freeing to her.

And though Tony was kind, and sexy, and she knew she was falling for him, he would never understand that side of her. Would he?

God, she needed a spanking. She *so* needed a spanking. Her hands shook, and for one brief minute she wished she smoked.

She needed something, *anything*, to calm her fraught nerves. She massaged her hands so roughly atop her scarred legs, it hurt.

Tessa rarely drank, and never smoked, but she had been a regular member of The Club now for a good, long while. Submitting to be spanked was her preferred method of stress relief.

Her plan had been to go to The Club a few days prior, before the onslaught of the weekend craziness. But Tony had been testing out a new recipe for Insalata de Carciofi, a raw artichoke salad with lemon and olive oil, in the kitchen at *Cara*. He'd been singing to classic Italian music in his adorable, off-key baritone, and he'd insisted he needed someone to taste-test. Before she knew it, they'd opened a bottle of wine, and hours passed while they talked and laughed. After that, he'd insisted on just taking her home. So it had been weeks since she'd been spanked, and she was craving it.

But still, everything would've been okay for a little while longer, if she hadn't had to go to her mother's house. An hour later, she was still quaking with the fury and helplessness that only Desiree Damon could make her feel.

She hadn't *wanted* to go. In fact, she'd had every freaking plan to never set foot in that hellhole again. But she had spent the morning hanging out with her sister, window shopping and drinking fancy pumpkin spice coffee before yet another of Nora's study groups, when Nora had remembered that she'd left her notes at home. Tess wasn't about to make the girl take the train all the way back home to get them, not when all she had to do was put her big girl pants on and drive her there.

But when she pulled up in front of the two-family house, her stomach clenched. She *hated* the apartment where she grew up.

"Let's make this quick," she said to Nora as she unbuckled her seatbelt.

"You don't have to come in!" Nora said, "I can just…"

Tessa felt bad making Nora go in alone. "It's fine. We just

won't stay longer than we have to. I don't want to even *look* at her, let alone whatever guy she's got this week."

"Mostly only one guy these days," Nora said looking out at the house with a sigh. "*Roger.*" Her voice was thick with disgust. "He's maybe thirty? Mom says he's *energetic* and makes her feel younger. Personally, I think it's probably the rainbow-colored stash of pills in his pocket that makes him energetic, not his youth."

Tess rolled her eyes. "Sounds charming!" Then her eyes narrowed. "Hey! How do you know what kind of pills he's got in his pocket?"

Nora looked uncomfortable. "Because he offered me some a few nights ago. I was up late writing a lab report for biology, and he said he knew something that could help me stay up."

Tess reached across the console and grabbed Nora's wrist. "Jesus, tell me you didn't take anything!"

Nora looked at her sister in disbelief. "God, Tess, of course I didn't! Do you really think after growing up in that house, watching mom strung out on one thing after another, that I would be that stupid?"

Tessa was instantly apologetic. "I know! I know. I'm sorry. I just… I worry so much about you living in that house."

Nora blew out a breath. "Yeah, I know you do. I wish you wouldn't, though! You have your own life to worry about. It's time I take care of myself! I'll be eighteen in a couple of months!"

Tess smiled halfheartedly. "I just wish you'd get to be a kid for a little while longer."

Nora's steady gaze met Tess's. "Neither one of us could ever really be kids growing up in *that*." She jerked her head at the house.

"Anyway," Nora said, shaking her head as if to clear away the bad thoughts and reaching for the door handle. "She's scheduled to be at work today, so hopefully we can get in and get out!"

Tess followed suit, and together they walked up the cracked concrete path, wishing their mother had a car to park in the driveway that might indicate whether or not she was home. Sadly, a car was not a luxury their mother could afford. Neither, some weeks, was soap. Or toilet paper. Or food.

This month, their mother was working as a checkout clerk at the grocery store and, fortunately for Nora, worked most afternoons. Who knew how long that would last, though? She hadn't been able to hold down a job for longer than six months for as long as Tessa could remember. Some of her boyfriends would occasionally chip in for bills, but most were losers who could care less. Tessa and Nora managed to squeak by. Mostly.

Tess inhaled as they went up the stairs, hoping they'd be lucky and the house would be empty.

They were not.

They knew the minute they opened the door to the entryway that someone was home because of the acrid cigarette smoke that stung their noses. Tessa's stomach churned with nausea.

"Don't talk to her," Nora whispered. "Don't even *talk* to her, Tess. I just need to grab my stuff from my room. God, I'm so stupid. I should've remembered it."

"Not your fault you left your things at your *home*, kiddo," Tess hissed back. "I promise, chickie. God, I promise, soon. Soon, you and I will be on our own."

Staying at Tony's had helped her sock money away. God, he paid for everything! And soon Nora would have a job at *Cara* too. Tony said he was going to interview her, though Tessa knew it was only a formality. He had already decided to hire her.

"I know it, Tess," Nora said, reaching for Tessa's hand and squeezing. "I can't wait."

When Nora opened the door to the first floor apartment on the left, the smoke hit their senses and Tessa reeled back.

"Well, look who decided to come home!" came their mother's slurred voice. "Where have you been?"

Before Nora could answer, a male voice purred, "Well, hey, Norrie. Don't *you* look *fine!*"

Tess stepped into the room behind Nora and her eyes flashed to the man sprawled on the couch next to their mother. He was young, as Nora had said, and all arms and legs—a gaunt mass of bones who was likely nearly six feet tall when he was standing... though he didn't look capable of standing at the moment. His hair was dirty blond and just plain *dirty*; his pale eyes were red-rimmed and watery above his beaked nose, and the blissful smile that stretched his lips revealed that he was missing more than one tooth.

Mom sure knew how to pick 'em.

But it was the way he was staring at Nora that had Tess's senses on high alert. He was eyeing her up like a chocolate sundae.

Her *baby* sister.

"Who are *you?*" Tess demanded, stepping in front of Nora.

The man shifted his leer in her direction.

"I'm Roger, baby. Who are *you?*"

"This here is my *other* daughter, Miss High and Mighty," her mother taunted. "Thinks her shit don't stink. She's not welcome around here."

"I thought you'd be at work today," Nora said nervously.

Desiree waved a hand in the air. "I quit. I don't need that place."

Nora shut her eyes. "Oh, Mom."

"It's not my fault!" Desiree protested. "Jimmy hired me. He was real laid back, understood how shit worked. New fucking cunt manager comes in and doesn't like the way I dress, wants me to pee in a fucking cup. Bull *shit*, I told her."

Nora shook her head, as if unable to speak. But really, what was there to say?

Tess made a mental note to stick some more grocery money in Nora's bag before she dropped her off.

"She looks too grown up to be your daughter, Desi," Roger said, still staring at Tess. His eyes had moved to her chest and he honest-to-God licked his lips.

Tess couldn't repress her shudder.

"I had her when I was practically a baby myself, Rog," Desiree whined, rubbing her hand on the man's emaciated thigh.

This was no more than the truth. In her younger years, Desiree had been a blonde beauty, with hair that hung in waves past her shoulders, and the same brown eyes and curvy figure as Tessa. According to the story she liked to tell, she'd fallen hard for Tess's father, who'd played guitar in a local band and had promised to marry her. Tess could neither confirm nor deny these details, since her father had barely stuck around long enough for the pregnancy test to turn blue. What she *did* know was that neither impending motherhood nor being kicked out of her parents' house had sobered her mother at all, and the last twenty-plus years of drugs, alcohol, cigarettes, and hard living had aged her prematurely. Her hair was now greasy and limp, her skin sallow and drawn, her eyes dull and lined.

"Don't look at her," Nora whispered, prodding Tess in the back as if to move her from the room. "Let's go!"

But Tess wouldn't budge. Roger, the weasel, was still eyeing her up like she was his dinner. She couldn't believe her mother would let someone like *this* live in the house with her teenaged daughter.

Oh, no, wait. Yes, she could.

Desiree seemed to realize that Roger's attention was firmly focused on Tess, and her face twisted in jealous anger.

"Why are you here, anyway?" she said, rising to her feet. "Coming to slum with us?"

Tessa ignored her and finally allowed Nora to prod her to the small windowless room at the back of the house that served as her bedroom, the bedroom they'd *shared* when Tess still lived there. Tess shivered when Nora reached around her and pushed the door open. Nothing had changed. It was still dark and coffin-like, containing nothing but two twin beds and an old table that served as a desk. Just being in this house again made her feel sick.

Nora grabbed the papers she needed from the desk, and towed Tess back into the hallway.

"Let's go," she whispered.

"Go? So soon?" their mother spat, and Tessa flinched. She hadn't realized they were followed.

"We need to get going," Tessa said, her teeth clenched. "Excuse me."

"No, excuse *me*," her mother said, her eyes shiny and unfocused. She swayed on her feet, but still managed to jab a finger in Tessa's chest so hard it hurt. "Nora's my daughter and you can't take her with you."

It figured that the only time her mother even cared that she *had* Nora for a daughter was when she could use her to taunt Tess.

"To her *study group*? The hell I can't," Tessa said. "Now *move.*"

Anger clawed at her chest, hot fury bubbling up at the woman who'd made her life a living hell.

Tessa reached out a hand to hold her mother back, but her mother moved faster than she'd thought possible, grabbing a fistful of Tess's hair and yanking hard. Tess screamed as pain radiated from her scalp. Instinctively, she elbowed her mother, and her mother howled, doubling over. Tess took both hands and shoved her away. The hallway was so narrow, her mother's body slammed against the wall.

"Get the hell away from us!" Tessa screamed. "Put a hand on me again, and I call the police!"

"Hey, hey, what's this?" Roger lumbered into the hallway, his eyes narrowed on them. "Desi, baby, we don't want any trouble, remember?" he warned.

Her mother was practically vibrating from fury and whatever cocktail of chemicals were currently working inside her, but she allowed Roger to step in front of her and hold her back against the wall, while Nora and Tess edged past.

"You think you're so much better than us now? You and your fancy car and fucking job?" Desiree screamed. "You think you can just sashay your way in here and you're fucking welcome?"

Tessa stopped when she was in front of her mother, and pointed a shaking finger at her. "I wouldn't come back here if it was the last fucking place on earth," she hissed. "I'm only here because of Nora. We're leaving."

"Get out, and don't come back!" her mother shrieked.

Nora took Tessa by the hand and yanked her out the door.

An hour later, Tessa was still shaking from the helpless anger. Nora was with her study group and already had plans to stay over her friend's house. But Tess had no means to get away.

God, what she wouldn't do to go over the lap of *someone*. Hell, *anyone*.

Her ex-boyfriend Louie was the one who'd introduced her to the scene. She'd met him when she was still in high school. He was five years her senior, and she had been drawn to his dominant personality. It had been over Louie's lap she'd gotten her first-ever spanking, and she'd never looked back. He showed her it was darkly erotic and freeing to give control to someone else. Louie hadn't exactly been into long term, though, and was still young and immature. He couldn't handle the responsibility of being a full-time dom. He liked to spank, and he liked to screw, but meeting the needs of a submissive was where he fell woefully short. Their break-up was amicable, and she'd always been grateful he had shown her a side of herself that had lain dormant.

She glanced at her phone. No time. She couldn't even go to The Club and ask one of the guys there for a quickie. She knew enough men who functioned as Tops that she could ask them to help bring her back to her senses. A good spanking would center her, relieve stress, and help her relax, and most of them were more than happy to lay her over a bench and give her a few good whacks. Unfortunately, her shift started in just a few minutes.

Tessa's hands shook as she put her phone back in her bag and lay her head back on her seat. The tears that threatened to fall were right there, right on the surface, and for one second…

She jumped at a knock on the passenger-side window. Sitting up quickly, she recognized the large frame of her boss before her eyes even adjusted to the bright light streaming in behind him. He opened the door.

"Sorry. Would've just opened the door but didn't want to scare the shit outta ya," he said, as he slid into the passenger seat. "You okay? You've been sitting out here for like half an hour."

God! She had? She was losing her mind.

"Yeah," she said, tipping her head back on the seat and closing her eyes. "It's been a really long afternoon."

She didn't trust herself not to cry, so she just shook her head.

"You need some time off?" he said softly, and the tenderness in his voice almost made the lump in her throat dissolve. "I can take it from here tonight."

"No, thanks, Tony," she whispered.

They sat in silence for a few minutes. It felt nice, just sitting here with him. She missed chatting with Eva, who was so into her boyfriend now, she never answered calls anymore. She couldn't confide in Nora, and Hillary would understand, but Hillary was waiting tables and not really free to listen as Tessa spilled her guts.

And then a thought crossed her mind. If Tony knew that Hillary and Heidi, who were normal, healthy, perfectly happy girls, liked to be spanked, would he accept that she did, too?

The hell with it.

"I could really use a trip to The Club," she said. She kept her eyes closed shut, and she could hear his sharp intake of breath.

"You need… something at The Club?" he asked, as if genuinely curious.

She laughed mirthlessly. "Yes. I do. I need a really good session," she said with a laugh.

"Session? As in, like, sex?"

She laughed out loud. He was so damn cute sometimes. "Sex is good," she said, opening her eyes and watching him closely for a reaction. "But what I really need is a good spanking."

He nodded slowly, working his jaw as he listened. God, the man could listen. She loved how he really *listened* to her.

"Did you… do something wrong?" he asked. "And you… feel like someone should punish you?"

She shook her head, still smiling. "Not this time, no," she said. "But getting spanked can be good stress relief."

His brow furrowed. "Stress relief? Letting someone smack your ass *relaxes* you?"

She sighed. "Oh, yes. It so can." She put her head back and closed her eyes again. "It releases feel-good hormones. And the act of giving up control, it does a lot for a girl. It's freeing, to just clear your mind for a while, and not have to worry about anything but submitting. And then taking the spanking, knowing I can handle it, makes me feel strong and powerful."

He was quiet for a minute before he spoke. "Want to tell me what makes you so stressed today?" he asked. The lump in her throat rose again.

Her voice dropped to a whisper. "I saw my mother."

He paused for a beat before he spoke. "Shit, Tess."

"I know," she whispered, and she felt tears sneak out from beneath her eyelids. She reached her hands back and over her head, forgetting for a minute that when she did, the hem of her skirt rose. She knew he saw the scars when he swore again.

"Tessa. Jesus, Tess, what happened to you?" Her eyes flew open, but it was too late, one of his huge, warm hands had already reached out, his index finger tracing the edge of the scar on the uppermost part of her right thigh. She shoved his hand away.

"Please, Tony. Don't." She swiped at the tears in her eyes. God, what would he *think* about her? She'd just talked to him about needing to be spanked, and now he was looking at her scars. He was a bright guy. He'd put two and two together.

Would he tell her to get help? Would he lecture her? Would he get all awkward and clam up?

For a moment he said nothing, as she cried quietly to herself, wiping her eyes. But then his hand reached out to hers, and squeezed. The next moment, he released her hand, and was opening the car door.

Oh, *God*. She really *had* done it. He really *did* see her for the freak that she was, and he was out of here. She wanted to take it all back, and put the wall back up. But she couldn't. There *was* no taking it back. He was leaving, and she—

But, no. He wasn't leaving. The next thing she knew, the driver's side door was opening, and he was taking her hand again. He pulled her out of the car, and she blinked up at him, baffled at the sight of him, the sun dipping behind him in the autumn sky, as he pushed one large hand out and shut the car door behind her.

"C'mere," he said gruffly, and he did what she'd been pining for since the first time she ever laid eyes on him. He pulled her into his chest, wrapping his arms around her so tightly it hurt. And when he did, the feeling of being safe and accepted overwhelmed her. He *was* every bit as strong, and warm, and comforting as she'd imagined he'd be. She cried real tears as he rocked and held her.

"They'll see us," she said in a wavering voice, as he hushed her.

"I don't care," he answered. "What are they gonna do? Tell the boss?"

She laughed through her tears. "Maybe they'll talk," she said.

"Let 'em talk," he growled, and the next thing she knew, he was lifting her face and his mouth was on hers, the taste of salty tears intermingling with their kiss. It was a brief kiss that lifted her to the tips of her toes, and when he released her, she blinked up at him.

"This could make the roommate thing a bit, um, awkward," she whispered.

"Then you'd better stop trying to seduce me."

She snorted, smacking her hand flat on his chest, as he turned her around and led her into the restaurant to start their shifts.

He laughed. "Wait, I thought *you* were the one who liked to be smacked around," he said, and she punched him hard on the arm.

"Tony, don't *even!*" she said, but she was laughing. If he was joking around with her, then he couldn't think she was *that* much of a freak... could he?

She felt as if something had shifted, but she didn't yet know what.

Chapter 4

The first few notes of Bruce Springsteen's *Thunder Road* pounded through the kitchen as Tony hefted dough out of the giant mixer and onto the stainless steel countertop. Saturday mornings alone in the kitchen were the absolute best. He could crank his tunes as high as he wanted and sing as off-key as he pleased—the bread dough was the only witness, and it never told tales.

And why the hell *wouldn't* he sing? His family was happy, things with the restaurant were going so well he was booking months in advance, and thanks to luck and his own careful maneuvering, he was the lucky son of a bitch who got to start and end each day seeing Tessa Damon's smile.

That smile, man. He was quickly growing addicted to it, along with everything else that was Tess—from the husky sound of her laugh, to the sparkle in her eye when she teased him, to the soft curve of her hip beneath his hand as they'd sat on the sofa watching television the night before.

Some dim corner of his brain, likely the part that remembered exactly how it had felt when shit exploded with Val, cranked out an automatic warning—*Turn back! You can't give her what she needs!* But he'd started tuning out that voice a few days ago, right around the time he'd found himself holding Tess in the alley, and brushing his lips over hers in a kiss that had begun as a sign of comfort and affection, but which had become so much more. The way she'd cried in his arms then relaxed against him afterward, her sobs giving way to breathy laughter as the tension left her body, suggested that just maybe he *could* give her what she needed. Or at least *part* of what she needed. As for the other parts…

He floured his hands lightly and began working the dough into a long rope as he contemplated.

He'd seen and (unintentionally) overheard enough of the way his brothers treated their ladies to know that there were certain unwritten rules to the relationship between a dominant and a submissive. For example, a submissive always had to speak respectfully to her dom (though Hillie, in particular, pushed her luck with this from time to time). She deferred to him on all major decisions. And she followed the rules that he set out, which usually had to do with her safety and well-being. When she broke any of those rules, he'd spank her.

The safety part, he was all-in with. He'd love to know that Tess was taking care of herself and wasn't doing stupid-ass shit, like sleeping in her damn car. He shook his head and gave the dough a vicious twist.

Then he frowned, because the rest of the gig was a much tougher sell. For one thing, the very thought of spanking her, of causing her pain, made his stomach clench. For another, he genuinely liked it when Tess gave him sass—the way she tossed her hair back, the cheeky tilt to her mouth. It made him hard as a rock, however un-dom-like that probably made him.

And he wasn't all about being a dictator, either. There were a few things in life he *knew*—how to cook, how to tie his tie, how to tell when someone was lying. On pretty much every other topic, he accepted that he wasn't an expert, and it didn't make his balls shrivel to admit it. In fact, he remembered his dad saying that it took a strong man to admit that he didn't know what he was doing, and a smart man to seek help.

Still, could he try to live with those things, be that kind of guy, if that's what it took to keep Tess happy?

He remembered the feeling of her lips beneath his, warm and pliant, and the answer came easily. *Hell, yes* he could try.

As he cut the dough with his left hand and rolled with his right in the practiced way his mother had taught him, he found himself singing along with The Boss.

"Come take my hand, we're heading out tonight to… Oh, Jesus!"

A startling burst of color flashed in his peripheral vision, and Tony spun to confront the intruder… only to find none other than Tess, herself, standing there staring at him, her candy-apple red sweater clinging to her truly impressive curves. Despite the pounding of his heart, he couldn't help but grin.

"The lovely Miss Damon! Didn't expect to see you here today! How are you this fine morning?" he asked, resuming his work with the dough.

Tessa did not look nearly as happy to see him.

"Tony, what the heck is this?" she asked, brandishing a piece of paper at him.

"Well, I can't see it if you keep moving it," he said reasonably, squinting at the paper.

"It's an email," Tess told him.

"Yup, that's just what I was gonna say," Tony agreed. And when she continued to stare at him, he continued, "So, are you gonna tell me what it says? Or should I guess?"

Tess's cheeks flushed and she inhaled through her nose as though she was counting to ten. Did it make him completely depraved that he found the sight of her like this arousing?

More importantly, did he care?

"It's an email from Alice," she said.

Tony looked at her blankly.

"Alice *Cavanaugh*," she repeated, as though this should mean something.

It didn't. Tony shook his head. "Okay, I'll bite. Who's Alice Cavanaugh?" he asked, covering the rolls and setting them to rise.

"She works at The Club. As a waitress." Tessa began.

"Ah, right! Her!" Tony said, snapping his fingers as he grabbed the bench scraper and started to clean up. "She's a friend of Matt and Hillary's. More a friend-of-a-friend kind of thing. I don't think Matt even mentioned her name when he told me about her. She's looking for a temporary, part-time gig, and Matt vouched for her, so I told him to give her our contact info and we'd see what we could do. We can find her some shifts during lunch or weeknights when she's not at The Club."

Call him a sap, but helping out a single mom trying to save up to buy Christmas presents for her kid was a no-brainer.

Tessa stared at him, crestfallen. "But… you said… I thought we agreed… *Nora*…"

Tony paused in the act of scraping flour off the counter and frowned at her in confusion. "Your sister? What about her? She's coming for an interview in…" He quickly checked the large clock on the wall. "Half an hour. You reminded me twice yesterday *and* left me a sticky note on the apartment door this morning."

Which had been mildly annoying, frankly, since he wasn't an absent-minded guy. Messy, maybe, but never absent-minded.

Tess threw her hands up. "How the heck do you propose we hire *both* of them?" she demanded, her tone adding a "*you idiot*" to the end of her speech, even though she didn't voice it.

He narrowed his eyes as he felt his temper rise. "Well, Tess, it generally starts with *me* telling them they're hired, and then *you* schedule them some shifts. What's the problem?"

"The *problem* is that we can't *afford* to hire *two* new employees! We can barely hire *one*. And you didn't even discuss it with me before you promised!"

He held up his hand to cut her off. "Okay, hold up. First of all, I haven't promised anyone anything."

"That's not what this email says!" she nearly shouted, waving the paper at him once more. "She says to thank us so much, and she's available to start work as soon as you need her!"

Tony shrugged. He *hadn't* promised, but since he'd fully intended to employ the woman anyway, it didn't matter much.

"Great. Let's get her in for an interview this week. And as for your second point," he said, talking over her when she began to object. "We *can* afford it. Christ, Tess, we had two organizations call just *yesterday* to request outside catering jobs for holiday parties, and I happen to know that John," he said, referring to their kick-ass pastry-chef, "has a bunch of outside jobs coming up, and he can use the help, too. We need to grow our staff if we want the business to thrive."

"We need to be *careful*, Tony, if we want the business to *survive!* We could've gotten by with the staff we have! We could have made it work!"

Yeah, they could've made it work, but it would've meant forcing both of them, and the rest of the staff, to work sixteen-hour days through the holidays. No way. Tess already seemed to work eighty hours a week, staying late every damn night and coming in, *like today*, on her off-days. She'd wear herself out!

Besides which, she was making it sound like he had a reputation for making bad business decisions, which he absolutely did *not*. He'd hired Tess so he wouldn't have to spend his days chained to a desk, not because he couldn't handle his business. His personal decisions might have been a bit suspect, but never his decisions about *Cara*. Since when did she worry about the survival of *his* restaurant?

He took a breath and fought for patience, trying to figure out the best way to explain, to communicate his reasoning, to help her see past her worry, to calm his own temper.

And then a thought occurred to him. Would *Dom* explain his

rationale for every choice he made? Did *Matteo* have to talk Hillary into doing what he wanted? If there was an upside to being a dominant, that was definitely it.

He looked at Tessa and shook his head once, firmly. "No," he told her.

She waited for him to continue, and her eyes widened when she realized he wouldn't.

"No? Just *no*? End of story?" she sputtered.

"Tessa, as far as I know, this is still my restaurant. You may be the manager, but I'm the *owner*. I appreciate your concern, but it's not something you need to worry about. And I don't defer to you when making decisions," he told her calmly. "Especially not when I'm choosing to hire a part time, *temporary* employee."

Tess was apparently too shocked to speak. She stared at him, her lush lips momentarily frozen into a perfect O.

"Please email Alice back and set up a time for her to come in this week," he told her, doubling down on his decision.

She looked away for a moment, as if to compose herself. When she looked back, her eyes were shuttered and her shoulders slumped.

"All right, Tony. If you're sure that's what you want," she agreed quietly.

Of course it was. And this was what she needed from him. For him to take control.

"It is," he assured her.

But as she slowly nodded and walked away towards her office, he wondered why it felt so damn wrong.

Twenty minutes later, Tony had cleaned the kitchen, turned off the music, and was sitting in his office trying his best to focus on work in spite of his surly mood, when Tess knocked on his open door.

"Hey, um… Nora's here," she told him. She kept her eyes down, looking somewhere between the front of his desk and the floor.

He frowned. What the hell was that about?

"Yeah, I've been expecting her. Bring her in," he said.

She nodded and turned away.

"Hey, Tess!" he called.

She turned back obediently, and he faltered. He hadn't really had anything particular to say, he'd just wanted to see her roll her eyes at him and smile, neither of which she did.

"Never mind," he said grumpily. "Just bring her in."

Tess nodded and departed without a word.

She returned a minute later, leading a miniature blonde version of herself nearly staggering under the weight of an enormous Red Sox backpack.

"Hey!" the mini-Tess said, extending her hand and gifting him with a bright smile the moment she walked in his office. "I'm Nora!"

Tony found himself smiling despite his mood—he couldn't help it. Tess's sister seemed to have all of Tess's spirit and energy, compressed into one small package.

"Nora, I'm Tony," he told her, coming around the desk to shake her hand.

Obviously introductions were unnecessary, because Nora was nodding enthusiastically.

"Oh, I *know*," she said. "Tess has told me so much about you already!"

Had she now? Well, that was interesting.

Tony stole a glance at Tess, but Tess was giving her sister a death glare. "Nora! This is a formal interview. Professional, remember?"

Nora flushed. "Right. Yeah. I mean, *yes.*" She cleared her throat nervously.

Tony rolled his eyes and waved a hand dismissively. "Meh. Formality is *so* overrated," he scoffed. "We're practically family."

Nora giggled.

Tess sighed.

"Thank you, Miss Damon," Tony told Tess. "Nora and I can take it from here."

Tess met his eyes, *finally*, and her own narrowed in surprise. "What do you mean?" she asked suspiciously.

He shrugged. "Nora is here for an interview. So, *I* am planning to interview her."

"Wait, I thought that *we* would talk to her. *Together*. Figure out hours and wages and—" She trailed off when she saw Tony shaking his head.

"But *you* already know her," he reminded Tess, taking her elbow and gently turning her around so she was facing the kitchen. "If she's going to be working for me, *I* need to know her." He gave Tess a gentle shove, valiantly trying not to notice the way the fabric of her jeans cupped the curve of her ass... and failing miserably.

"Tony!" she said, whirling around and glaring at him. "But, I—"

He shut the door gently but firmly, cutting off her protest, and turned to face Nora. He clapped his hands together once and waggled his eyebrows. "So, Nora, let's talk."

Tony grabbed a folding chair from the corner, unfolded it in front of his desk, and motioned for her to take a seat. Nora giggled as she sat.

"Okay, I've never seen anyone handle Tess that way," Nora said. "That was kinda funny. Usually Tess is the one telling *me* what to do!"

"Tell me about it," Tony groused as he took his seat on the other side of the desk. "I have not one but *two* older brothers. I know a thing or two about bossy older siblings!"

Nora tilted her head to the side and frowned. "Well, I guess it's not *bossiness* with Tess, exactly. It's more like she's just worried about me 'cause she loves me."

Tony pretended to consider this. "Hmm. Nah, my brothers are just bossy," he deadpanned, making Nora giggle again.

"So, why is she worried about you?" he asked, steepling his hands on the desk.

Nora seemed to catch herself. "Ah, no particular reason. Just the usual teenage stuff," she hedged, shrugging one shoulder. She peered at him closely and continued, "Plus, our mom... Do you know about..."

Tony nodded shortly. "Tess has mentioned some stuff," he said. Just enough to make him wanna lock Tess in a bubble and never let her have contact with the woman. "You don't need to tell me specifics." He wanted Tess to tell him, in her own time.

Nora nodded, relieved. "It's just, you know, Tess looks out for me. Making sure I get my homework done, making sure I get decent food, making sure I've gotten my college applications in, that kind of thing. I don't think I appreciated it as much when I was younger, but now I see how much it costs her. Like, *literally*," she said ruefully.

Tony's attention was caught. "What do you mean?"

"Well, um, a few weeks ago I needed money for books and test fees and my mom, she... Uh. Well. Anyway, Tess helped out. Like, a *lot*," Nora admitted. "If I hadn't had that money, I would've been kicked out of the accelerated program at school, and then I could kiss my scholarship chances goodbye. I don't know what I would've done without her." Love and something like hero worship shone in Nora's face.

Christ. He'd figured it was some kind of emergency that had made Tess abandon her plan of moving into her own apartment, but he hadn't wanted to ask. Now he could see why Tess hadn't volunteered.

"But that's why I really want a job," Nora continued

earnestly. "I'm old enough that I can make money for myself and not have to rely on her anymore. Or at least not as much."

"I hear you," he told Nora. "You want to be your own person, take care of yourself."

Nora nodded.

"But your sister loves you. I'm sure she'll always be worrying about you and looking out for you in one way or another," Tony told her. "At least that's the way it is with my brothers." God help him.

"Probably. When Tess cares, she kinda can't help but worry!" Nora laughed. "It's how she shows her love."

Tony chuckled.

"You know, I was kinda worried that no one was looking out for *her*," Nora admitted. "But then she told me about all the things you've done to help her."

Tony frowned. *All* the things? What had he done? "You mean having her stay at my place?" he asked. "That's not a big deal. She's paying rent." Theoretically. And that was *all* he'd let her pay for.

Nora smiled. "Well, that, yeah. But also how you take care of her. How you listen to her when she talks, and respect her opinions. She feels safe with you. I mean, she doesn't exactly say it like that, but I can tell. And where we grew up, it wasn't exactly, um… stable. You know? So Tessa can cope with whatever the world throws at her. She's wicked strong. But it's nice that she doesn't have to."

Tony nodded, and his memory flashed to the scars on Tess's legs. Had that been her coping mechanism? And his conscience prickled. He hadn't exactly listened to Tess or respected her opinion today, had he? But ultimately, having him in control was what she wanted. Wasn't it?

He cleared his throat and focused his attention on Nora, giving her a warm smile. "Okay, enough chit chat. You've impressed me already."

"I have?" Nora asked, her face scrunched up in look so identical to Tess's look of confusion that Tony nearly laughed. "Oh! You mean because I mentioned my advanced classes?"

Tony *did* laugh this time. Like Tess, Nora had no idea the effect her sweet, loyal personality had on people.

"Yup, that was it, kiddo. That, and your Red Sox backpack," he told her with a wink. "Can't turn down a Sox fan. So let's talk money and hours. You're a minor, so there are some limitations about when you can work, and you'll need a work permit. If I know your sister, she has all that information printed out in triplicate already, so why don't I put her out of her misery and call her in here?"

Nora hesitated, then bit her lip. "Um, for the work permit form, do you think *you* can sign it for me, as my employer?"

Tony frowned. "Well, yeah, either Tess or I will have to sign it first, as your employer, saying what hours you'll work. And then you'll take it and—"

"Can *you* do it?" she interrupted in a whisper. "Specifically *you*? Because my mom won't mind me getting a job, but if she sees Tess's name, she, uh… might not sign it. She says Tess is a bad influence. I don't want Tess to know."

Tony blew out a breath. He could see that Nora was mortified to admit this, so he didn't want to vent any of the fury roiling around inside him and make her feel worse, but it took everything he had to swallow it down. He had never met Tess's mother and prayed he never would, but he knew for sure that Tess deserved better. How the hell had such an amazing person come out of that shitty situation?

"Sure, kiddo," he told Nora. He stood and stepped forward to open the door and call Tess. As he passed her, Nora shot him a nervous look, and he smiled encouragingly. "Don't worry. I'll take care of everything."

Somehow.

Tony had lived alone for a number of years, and he'd liked it that way. He was a gregarious person by nature, which was probably why he thrived in the restaurant business. But as the youngest of three kids in a large and boisterous family, he'd also always craved little pockets of quiet so he could relax and recharge.

He'd never dreamed that silence could be so crushing and oppressive.

It had been two hours since he'd arrived home from the restaurant, and at least an hour since Tess had gotten back from dropping Nora home after her interview. Tess was cooking something in the kitchen, but somehow Tony couldn't seem to settle to a task. He couldn't focus on the baseball game, or the book on his Kindle. All he could hear was the ringing *silence* where Tess's voice and laughter should have been.

It was fucking annoying.

Was she pissed off? Was she giving him the silent treatment? He couldn't even tell. Val's way of settling an argument had been to get in his face and make ultimatums. His brothers generally used their fists. His mother had only ever needed to *look* at him a certain way to express her anger.

And if Tess *was* pissed at his high-handedness, what should he do? Fight with her? Punish her? Spank her ass? Was that what a *dominant* would do? He hadn't the first fucking clue.

Yeah, she'd questioned his ability to do his job, and she'd been disrespectful about it. He expected better from her.

But all he knew for sure was that, looking back at his own behavior, he'd been rude, insensitive, and way out of line, speaking to her the way he had. They weren't in a formal D/s relationship—hell, they weren't in a relationship at *all*, for God's sake! - and she'd been trying to do her job. It wasn't her fault that wanting her so badly was fucking with his head. His own moral code demanded that he admit he was wrong and ask forgiveness.

And if that made him weak or whatever? Then fuck it. He'd go back to being a dominant tomorrow. For tonight, he just wanted peace in his mind and in his home.

He hauled himself off the sofa and stalked toward the kitchen.

"So... Nora's a good kid," he said offhandedly as he opened the refrigerator and grabbed a beer.

Tess, still in her red sweater and tight jeans, was standing barefoot at the sink, washing produce. She turned her head for one brief moment to acknowledge his presence, before turning her eyes back to the grapes in the colander.

"She sure is," Tess agreed proudly. "Did she tell you she was taking advanced classes?"

"Uh, yeah. She mentioned that."

Tony leaned back against the counter and took a deep drink. "So, about earlier," he began, not sure exactly what he planned to say.

"Yeah," she said. "About that."

As Tony exhaled and rubbed the back of his neck, struggling for words, Tess wiped her hands on a dishtowel and slowly turned to face him.

"I'm really sorry," she said, biting her lip. "You're the owner of *Cara* and I'm not. I was wrong to question you and I shouldn't have done that. I apologize."

He frowned. Wait. *What?*

"Tess," he began, shaking his head, "that's not—"

"Please," she said, pressing her hands to her stomach. "Just let me finish."

He nodded reluctantly and set his beer on the counter.

"I expressed myself badly earlier. I didn't mean to imply that I don't trust you. I do. I just... worry. It's stupid, but sometimes I can't help it." She offered him a half-smile, and Nora's words came flashing back to him.

When Tess cares, she can't help but worry. It's how she shows her love.

Jesus. Could he be a bigger jerk than he already was? She hadn't been doubting his ability to run things, she'd been giving him shit about the restaurant because it was *important* to her. And hadn't she proved that, time and again, by working like crazy trying to make things better? She'd been scared, and instead of explaining his reasoning and comforting her, he'd gotten pissed off.

Well done.

"And when I think of all you've done for me and now for Nora," she continued. "I owe you so much, and know I'll never be able to repay you. The very least I can do is be a good employee."

"Stop," he said roughly.

"No, really, Tony! I've been thinking about this all day."

"Stop!" he said more forcefully. He strode forward and grasped her elbows gently. "I don't ever want to hear you talk like that again."

Her lower lip trembled. "I won't. I'm really…"

"Not *that*," he said, shaking her gently. "I don't ever want to hear you say that you *owe* me. You don't owe me a damn thing."

"But," she argued.

"Never. Again," he said firmly. "Do you understand?"

She nodded, wide-eyed.

"You do the work of three people at the restaurant. Which is why I *know* that we need more than Nora's help to get us through the busy season. You work too hard, Tess," he told her, lifting a hand to stroke his thumb gently over her cheekbone.

Her eyes widened impossibly further, and she swallowed hard. "I do?"

He nodded.

"And that's why you want to hire Alice?"

He nodded again. "And I should have explained that."

She shook her head. "You shouldn't have to justify—"

His free hand moved from her elbow to her waist, and he

pulled her firmly towards him so that their chests nearly touched. "No, you're right. I don't have to justify my decisions to my manager. But you're not just my manager."

She looked at him with wide, hopeful eyes. *Shit.* Why had he waited so long? "I should have taken the time to *explain* it so that *you* would have what *you* need from me. And for that, *I* am sorry."

She swallowed again, her breathing choppy. "Okay," she agreed.

Her ragged reply made him smile. "My only excuse is that I've been incredibly distracted all day, all *week*, thinking about you."

"Have you? About me, uh…" Her arms rose to loop around his neck, her fingers driving into his hair in a way that made him close his eyes and stifle a groan. "Working too hard?"

"No, Tessa," he told her, his voice a barely-intelligible growl even to his own ears. "About your beautiful eyes, and your gorgeous smile, and about the way your ass fills out these jeans."

The hand at her waist deliberately moved down, and then in, cupping her ass, and pulling her pelvis flush against him, so that the hard length of him pressed into her belly.

He hissed in pleasure. Tess moaned.

"I'm going to kiss you now, Tess," he informed her, grabbing her hands and raising them above her head while he backed her against the refrigerator door.

"That'd be good," she agreed, struggling against his hold, trying to get her hands back on him.

He grinned. He might suck at the other dominant stuff, but this part was second nature.

He stepped forward, bracing one leg between hers, and leaned down to whisper in her ear. "And when I do, I'm not going to stop. Understand?"

"Tony, please," she said, her brown eyes wide and unfocused, her hips lifting instinctively, trying to make contact with his.

"Do you *understand*?" he demanded.

"Yes! Yes, sir! I do!" she cried.

Fuck yes.

Sir.

The thrill of it went through him, an electric jolt that rocketed up his spine and had him pulling her arms higher, holding her wrists even more firmly. One simple word, but it changed everything.

He wouldn't stop until he'd made her his.

Chapter 5

This wasn't happening. It was some sort of surreal dream, and someone would pinch her to wake her up, because good things like this did not happen for Tessa Damon. You had to claw, fight, and push your way to the top to get things to happen. It took blood, sweat, and tears.

And Tony was so *good*. How could someone like Tessa be what Tony wanted? The night of Heidi and Dom's wedding, the two of them had been alone in the dark, having taken their champagne flutes out to where the small waterfall ran behind the terrace, and he'd been still reeling from his break-up with Val.

"I want a good girl, Tess," he'd told her. "Not a prima donna. I want a girl I can raise my kids with. Someone wholesome, and pure. A good girl."

She'd replayed his words over and over again.

She was not a good girl.

But what sort of fool would take what she wanted so badly, and hand it back? And Tony did strange things to her willpower. Her resolve would melt away and she'd be left with her burning need to be near him, to touch him, to feel his hands on her, and she'd shove down any self-doubt that threatened to ruin her euphoria.

If he ever knew who she really was, he wouldn't be pinning her against the refrigerator right now, his hands on her waist and curves, as his huge, rough hands shoved her sweater up and his fingers grazed the edge of her naked skin above her jeans. If he knew what she'd done, where she came from, and who she was, he would not be with her right now. Not ever. He'd drop her, like every other goddamn guy she'd ever let in. And as his tongue met hers, she let out a half-moan, half-sob that she hoped he mistook for wanton need, not the tortured bundle of doubts that strangled her.

"Tony," she whispered, pulling her head back and placing her hands on his broad shoulders, lifting up on her tiptoes to anchor herself on him while his hands spanned her waist. She squirmed. God, the feel of those hands. Nothing, *nothing* could prepare her for what it felt like to be held by him. The mere touch of his hands on her made her skin feel red hot and too tight. Hell, she'd barely been able to manage focusing on the movie they'd watched the night before because his massive hand had spanned her waist. It was comforting. Consoling. And so very sexy. She'd sat next to him panting, squirming, hoping there was no way he had some sort of superpower that enabled him to detect her damp panties and labored breathing that being in near proximity to him brought out in her.

She was ashamed of how easily he turned her on. Whereas other girls might welcome the arousal, she felt as if her body betrayed her, and it was a harsh reminder of how many men she'd lain on her back to please.

"You'd spread your legs for anything that walked," her mother had growled at her one night, in a drunken rage, after catching Tessa with her boyfriend on the living room couch.

Tony was too good.

Too good.

"We can't… I can't… Tony," she said, pleading, her hands on his shoulders. She stared at the way his shoulders spanned her hands, strong, and indomitable. Being overpowered by him like this made her feel small and in need of protection, and he seemed so very happy to provide that.

He leaned in and kissed her cheek, a soft, gentle touch that made tears well in her eyes and her throat catch.

"Tony..." she whispered again. How could she say it? How could she tell him what she needed to?

"What is it, Tess?" he whispered in her ear. "I don't care that we work with each other. I wouldn't have asked you to move in here if I didn't want you to. And we can make this work, Tessa. If it's too much too soon, I get it, honey." He sighed into her ear, his hand teasing caressing her breast in a move so tender, it made her desire for him impossibly stronger. He was so *good*.

"I can't, Tony," she said. "If you only knew." It was now or never. She would spill all, before they reached the point of no return, before it was too late. "You can't do this with me." She lifted her chin and inhaled. "I'm not who you think I am."

He pulled back and frowned, and her eyes watered with unshed tears. His eyes narrowed on hers and he'd never looked so stern. She fairly quaked as he reached for her chin and tilted her eyes to his.

"What exactly is that supposed to mean?" he whispered low.

God, Tess! God! Take everything you've ever wanted and just throw it out, why don't you?

But she *had* to. For *him*.

"I've... I'm not a good girl, Tony." Her voice wavered and the tears finally spilled. "You said you want a good girl. I'm not a good girl. I'm not who you want or need."

He gave her a long, piercing look, and she wanted to turn away, or run, but something in her said *stay*.

"What do you mean?" he whispered.

Shame heated her face as she whispered back. "I've been with many guys, too many. So, so many. The first time I ever had sex was in the back of my high school boyfriend's pick-up truck.

He had a dirty blanket in the back and a cheap condom in his wallet." She closed her eyes as she continued. "I've been tied up and whipped in clubs. I've had sex in public, and with more than one person at a time. I was sex slave to a master at the club for a full year before he left me for another submissive. I wasn't good enough. I've never been good enough, and I—"

She felt a finger come to her lips, and she stopped, her eyes opening.

And when he spoke, his voice wasn't harsh, angry, or, worse, disgusted. It was so soft and gentle, the knot in her chest began to loosen.

"Tessa Damon," he whispered, his hands reaching for her hips and drawing her close to him. "Do you want to know what *I* think?"

She nodded, not trusting herself to speak.

Please.

Let me go before I make things worse.

Make it better.

He pulled her head to his chest and kissed the top of her head in a move so tender, she closed her eyes against the power of it. He leaned down and whispered in her ear.

"I think you and I have two very different ideas of what *good girl* means."

It was the last thing she expected him to say, and the very thing she needed to hear. She lifted her face off his chest and went up on her tiptoes to kiss him.

He kissed her in earnest now, his lips moving in time to hers, as his hands went back to her waist and he pulled her forward with him. Moving across the room, he hoisted her onto the counter with one quick move. She wrapped her legs around him as he yanked her shirt over her head, revealing full breasts in a scarlet, lace-edged bra. He moaned, dropping his gaze to her breasts, he removed her bra. Seconds later, his mouth dropped, and he was teasing her nipples with his tongue. Her head fell back and her legs clenched tighter around him. He lazily pressed a thumb between her legs, circling and teasing until she felt as if she'd climax right there on the counter of the kitchen.

"Come with me, baby," he whispered, wrapping her legs around him and walking to the couch carrying her. He laid her down as he knelt above her, his hands going to the edge of his t-shirt and lifting. She'd only caught a glimpse of him bare-chested when he came out of the shower, but now she unabashedly stared. God, his chest. He wasn't chiseled and buff, but naturally defined, massive across the shoulders, so strong.

"Take off your jeans," he said. "Jesus, babe, are those *painted* on?"

She giggled. She did so love these jeans. Unzipping her jeans, she shimmied them off gratefully as he unfastened his buckle.

Tessa swallowed, momentarily transfixed on his belt as he removed it, first unfastening the buckle, then pulling it through the loops of his jeans. He doubled it over in his hands and tossed it to the floor. She watched every move.

His eyes met hers and he grinned.

"You seem to be attracted to my belt, Miss Damon," he teased. She swallowed. Aw, the hell with it.

"Yes, sir." He chuckled, but when his eyes dipped to her barely-clothed body beneath him, he stared. Her scars.

Fuck, her scars. She closed her eyes, but his voice made her flutter them open again.

"Look at me," he ordered. She obeyed. He dropped down, his large, warm body pressed up against her, his erection against her belly as his mouth dipped down. "Open your legs," he ordered and she obeyed.

"Good girl," he whispered. "Such a good girl." He kissed her belly, then down to her thighs, and he kissed each leg in turn, first her left leg, scars and all, then her right. "You like doing what you're told, baby?" he asked.

She nodded. "I do," she whispered.

He nodded, one hand reaching to her satin panties and dipping a finger in between her legs, the only thing keeping him from her sensitive folds the small strip of satin between her legs.

"Let's see," he whispered. "What would you like to see me do to you, Tessa?"

He reached one finger below the edge of her panties and stroked a finger lazily.

"That's nice," she whispered. He chuckled.

"You want me to touch you?" he said, lifting his finger up and she arched her hips closer to him, groaning in protest. "That's it? Just touch you? That's all you want?" He reached a hand out to her elbow and touched her. "Done. I touched you."

She groaned.

"You don't want me to do anything else?"

Tessa nodded.

"Tell me."

She lifted her arm up over her head, drunk on arousal and the relief he brought her, and her words came all out in a rush. "I want you to lick me, and fuck me, and tie me up, and spank me, and push me to my knees and make me suck you off," she whispered.

He chuckled darkly. "All at once?" he said.

"Whenever, however, whatever," she moaned. God, her need for him was mounting with every second.

"I've never spanked a girl," he said, lazily stroking along the edge of her panties. Just hearing Tony say *spank* made her panties dampen. She shoved her legs together. He sobered. "Does it turn you on, Tessa?"

She nodded, licking her lips. "So much," she whispered. "Oh, God, the thought of being stretched across your lap," she said. She needed a spanking *so bad*, and there was no one in the world she'd rather surrender to than Tony. "The total feeling of letting go… knowing you're strong enough to do that, it feels…" and then she remembered who she was talking to, and had all those things that were going through her brain really just come out of her mouth?

"But it's okay," she quickly amended. "I know it's not your thing. We could try other things…"

Her voice trailed off, as he pulled away from her and sat on the sofa next to her feet.

"Come here," he ordered.

Oh my God. Oh my *God!*

She sat up, hardly able to breathe for the pounding of her heart, her hands clammy and moist as she sat up.

"Over my lap?" he asked. Oh God, he was gonna do it. He really was. She was more nervous and more turned on than the times she'd been spanked by masters at The Club, and some of those guys knew how to spank. This was different, because… well, this was Tony.

He gave her a stern look. "I've never done this before, but I'm pretty sure if I tell you to come over here, you're supposed to do what I say. Right?" She blinked.

Whoa. Yes, *sir*.

Licking her lips, she nodded while she scooted over to him. He smiled, holding her hand, and her belly melted. He furrowed his brow.

"Am I supposed to smack you hard enough to make you cry?"

Oh, he was adorable.

She shrugged. "Well… yes and no," she said. "But not always. I don't usually cry, especially for a sexy spanking. If I were in trouble…"

His jaw tightened. "I'm not punishing you, Tessa," he said, and she nodded, but it didn't disappoint her the way she thought it would. Though she wanted him to be stern and demanding with her, and she fantasized about naughty girl spankings, the fact that he was doing this his own way was a turn-on somehow.

"Of course not," she said. "I get that. It's just…"

But the words died on her lips as he sobered. He was patting his lap.

"Look, just because I've never done this doesn't mean I won't," he said. "We're not talking about me making you obey me. We're talking about spanking you because it turns you on, and you want me to give it a shot. Yeah?"

She nodded, her throat dry. She tried to speak, but the words became all jumbled. "I... you... we..."

"Then stop talking and show me how this is done," he ordered. "I know some guys use things to spank with, but I figure if these hands are big enough to pound out bread dough, they're big enough to spank your ass." He patted his lap again. "Now what are you waiting for?"

Her heart hammered in her chest. Now was the time. This was her chance. And she was not going to fuck this up. Tentatively, she laid herself over his lap, her belly on the warm breadth of his legs, his thighs hard beneath her bare skin. Her hands shook as she placed them on the floor, and when his large hand rested gently on her panty-clad bottom, her thighs constricted, his touch sending waves of arousal between her legs. One stroke of his finger, one lick of his tongue, was all it would take.

"Tell me what you need," he said, his voice so gentle, it seemed almost ironic he was talking about spanking her. His gentleness made the tears threaten to fall again, her throat clogged with them. She'd been bossed around and tied up, ordered into submission and whipped, but never had any of the men she was with asked her not only what she wanted, but what she *needed*.

"A real spanking," she whispered. "One that hurts. I want to feel your strength."

One of his hands wrapped around her waist, and her hand instinctively flew back. He grasped it, holding her hand, a gesture that was at once intimate and assuring, pressing her hand, engulfed in his large one, into the small of her back as the first smack of his hand fell. Her panties were thin and his hand large; the sting from the single swat hurt more than she'd expected.

"Ow," she said in a little voice.

"Too hard?" he asked, squeezing her hand in the small of her back.

"Noooo, no no no, please, Tony," she said. "Not too hard. That's *perfect*."

Another sound smack jolted her, and now he was spanking her in earnest, his palm rising and descending, and the heat of each spank warmed her skin, beginning with a jolt of pain that quickly spread to warmth, and her clit zinged with each stroke. To her immense pleasure, she felt his erection, hard as a rock beneath her belly.

He paused, and she almost cried. She wanted more, needed more, but it was okay if he was done now because moving onto other things would be—

But no.

He'd only paused to lower her panties.

"Bare skin," he said. "I want to feel your bare skin."

She squeezed his hand, as he continued to speak, his voice low and soothing. "You tell me if this is too much, honey."

Too much? Oh, God, she could stay here *forever*.

"Not too much," she whispered. "I'll take what you give me."

Another squeeze of his hand in hers, and his right hand rose, descending with a sharp crack that echoed through the apartment. She moaned out loud, squirming against his lap. He spanked her again, and she involuntarily jolted, but he did not stop. He gave her another sound swat, and another. Her skin was aflame. She was so turned on she could do nothing but squirm and moan, which only encouraged him further.

After several rounds of good, hard swats, he spoke. "That's enough for now," he said low, one hand resting on her fiery hot bottom, the other still holding her hand against the small of her back as he gently caressed her. She stood, pulling her panties up, and crawled into his lap as she'd longed to do. She sat on his thighs as his arms encircled her. She leaned in and kissed him, one hand trailing along the rough edge of his stubbled chin, the other placed on his bare chest. He returned the kiss, and when he pulled back, his voice was rough and husky.

"Get to my bed. *Now.*"

She stood and trotted to his room, feeling him in hot pursuit behind her, and another stinging swat landed on her bottom that had her squealing.

"Get those off," he growled, one large finger pointing accusingly at the panties that shielded her otherwise naked body from his gaze. She obeyed as quickly as her fingers would allow, nimbly stripping and looking to him for guidance. Did he want her on her back? Knees? But her questions evaporated as he reached the bed, guiding her gently but firmly against the pillows, nestling her head back and kissing her as he lowered himself between her legs. He paused for one quick moment to remove his boxers and then he was back, holding her wrists firmly in one hand while the other reached into his nightstand drawer and removed a condom.

"Hurry!" she begged.

His answer was a growl. He tore the foil open with his teeth, then leaned back and covered himself.

A moment later he was sliding between her legs.

He felt so right. She'd been with so many men she'd lost count, men who knew how to fuck and those who didn't, men who played her body like an instrument and those who hadn't, but never had she been with a man who was strong yet gentle, and the experience of making love to Tony made her feel different. He wasn't just in it for the sex. He didn't just want her ample breasts and pussy. He cared about *her*, Tessa, had seen her scars and kissed them, spanked her because she wanted him to, and even now, as he laid her down, he made sure her head was atop a pillow and the weight of him over her was tempered.

She'd had sex with guys. But she'd never made love to a real man.

He thrust into her, and she moaned, her bottom still stinging and warm, as his hot, powerful body moved in and out, filling her, and it felt so perfect being as close to him as possible. Every thrust of his hips shot spasms of ecstasy through her body, until she finally climaxed so hard, he held her hips down as she came. He was mere seconds behind her, his groans oddly pleasing to her, knowing that *she did that to him*.

His head fell to her chest, and they panted together. She trailed one hand along his dampened back, then trailed back to his hair, twirling a finger and lifting her mouth to his massive shoulder. She kissed him tenderly.

"How'd I do?" he said in a teasing whisper, his lips grazing the top of her breast with a kiss.

"Oh, not bad," she lied, as they both well knew that was fucking amazing. "Not too bad for a trial run. But you know, they say practice makes perfect."

He chuckled and landed a quick swat to her thigh. She giggled, wondering exactly what the hell had just happened.

They lay in the darkness. He'd padded out to the kitchen and retrieved the grapes she'd left in the strainer, snagged a container of sliced cheddar, and a box of pretzels. Tony covered her in a sheet, and they nibbled on the snacks, as he talked to her about growing up with Dom and Matteo, their mother who fed them as if they'd been starving waifs in a third world country, and the first time Matteo had revealed to Tony that he and Dom were into the BDSM scene.

"What'd you think?" Tessa asked, swirling a finger through the curly hair on Tony's chest as she watched him talk, the sound of his voice soothing and melodic. He plucked a grape from the vine and lifted it to her lips. She opened her mouth, sucked in the grape, and he swallowed. She watched his Adam's apple bob up and down as he plucked another grape and fed it to her.

"I thought he was crazy," Tony said with a chuckle. "And I had no idea where our mama had gone wrong. She raised us to be gentlemen, and to treat women like ladies. It seemed so wrong to me."

She nodded. "I get it," she whispered, noting his use of the past tense. "You don't think it's wrong anymore?"

He shook his head with a chuckle. "How could I? Somehow, my entire social circle is comprised of these strong, intelligent, happy people who are into this shit." She smiled. He was right. Matteo and Hillary, Heidi and Dom, their pastry chef John and his boyfriend Paul, and Tessa herself. "So I've accepted for a while that this was all normal and natural, just not my thing."

Was it still not his thing? She was afraid to ask, but it was something she needed to know. They'd just had amazing sex, and now they were hanging out like the friends they were, talking about their family, and nibbling on snacks, and when the sheet dipped down over her shoulder, he tucked it back over her.

"Not because I don't like the view," he said, with a groan. "Just don't want you to get cold." He was so *good*.

Still, could she be with Tony, as her lover? The submissive side of her wasn't something she could just turn off and tune out. Tessa Damon was not someone who hid who she was, or who caved to fear. No. Swallowing, she pushed herself up and sat on the bed, cross-legged, draping the sheet around her. She lifted her chin and inhaled deeply, as he shoved a handful of pretzels in his mouth.

"So," she said. "You say you don't think it's wrong anymore. Do you think... this is something you could get used to?"

His eyes widened as he swallowed. "Spanking you?"

She nodded, biting her lip, not even realizing she was holding her breath.

He grinned. "Girl, that was just about the hottest thing I've ever done."

She could've clapped her hands in glee.

"*Reeeally?*"

"Hell yeah. God, that was scorching hot. The way you lit up that way... seeing you squirm over my lap... yeah." He cleared this throat, and sobered. "I could see the appeal."

She smacked his arm.

"Pervert."

He chuckled. "At your service."

She reached a hand out for a grape, and he shook his head, placing it on the tip of her tongue himself. She smiled, chewing the grape.

"Thank you," she whispered, suddenly overcome with emotion. "I... told you that stuff about me, and you didn't push me away. You said it was okay anyway. You know things about me and you didn't run away."

His hand froze over the bag of pretzels, and his brows furrowed. He sat up across from her, shifting on the bed so he was sitting up straighter. "Tessa." She nodded, her heart pounding. Where was he going with this? Why had he grown so serious, all of a sudden?

"Do you mean to tell me you've told people about yourself, and people have turned *away* from you?"

She lowered her eyes to her hands and nodded. "Most of them," she whispered.

"Sonofabitch," he mumbled. "What a goddamned stupid thing to do."

She shrugged. "No one wants to get in bed with a fucked up chick, Tony."

To her surprise, his eyes darkened and he pursed his lips. "Tessa, you know I'm not into the 'spanking as punishment' thing," he said. "But talking about yourself that way just might make me change my mind."

Her heart thumped in her chest and she closed her eyes. He had no idea how he was touching on every single nerve in her body. The way his voice dropped low, and he mentioned spanking her, but most of all, the way he *cared* about her.

"Okay," she whispered. One curt nod indicated he'd made his point, so she changed the subject.

"So yeah. My mother's an abusive alcoholic and Nora still lives there, but she's never home anymore."

Tony nodded, but his eyes were cloudy. "She hit you?"

Tessa nodded and bit her lip. He swore under his breath, as she continued. "When I was in high school, I got into self-harming. It was scary, and dangerous, and somehow, gave me control when I felt everything in my life was spiraling out on me." Inhaling, she continued. "I would take a knife or razor, and cut myself until I bled. Somehow the adrenaline surge from it was addictive."

He nodded.

"I don't do that anymore," she whispered.

"How long?"

"It's been a few years."

"Are you still tempted?"

Her voice dropped. "All the time. There were two things that helped me escape the life I hated," she said. "Cutting myself, and sex. I don't cut myself anymore. I haven't in years. And submitting to a spanking at The Club helped for a time, but I haven't done that in a while now either."

He nodded. "I get it." He reached a hand out and tucked a stray piece of hair behind her ear. "Look how far you've come."

How far *had* she come?

He continued. "You've got a career now. You've got a job you're damn good at, friends who love you." He paused. "And a really sexy boss, who's your boyfriend."

Boyfriend. She liked the sound of that but needed to tease him first.

She giggled and punched his shoulder. "Sexy boss, huh?"

"Hey!" he said, rubbing his shoulder. "Is it okay for you to punch the guy who spanked you? Doesn't that earn you, like, more spanks or something?"

She giggled harder, and punched his other shoulder. "Depends on what the rules are."

"Now you're really asking for it," he said, leaning over and pushing her over on the bed, pinning her wrists by her side. "Do that again, and you're gonna get it."

She squirmed as he tickled her. "Hey," she said. "Seriously, dude! Will you spank me again?"

"Oh, you can count on it," he said. "Whether or not that's sooner than later is entirely up to you."

She squealed.

But even as she felt him hold her, and she felt impossibly aroused again, she couldn't help but wonder.

What would go wrong next? Good things did not happen to Tessa Damon.

She didn't deserve a guy like Tony.

When would he realize he was making a horrible mistake?

Chapter 6

Tony entered his apartment building, shutting the door behind him. He leaned back against it, contemplating the stairs in front of him with a heavy sigh. *Nearly home.* The neighbors were having a party, if the pounding bass and loud laughter were any indication, but he was not remotely tempted to socialize. Just one flight up and he could flop into his bed, preferably with his gorgeous girlfriend in a glorious repeat of last Saturday night, and forget this whole damn day.

"Hey, Mama, remind me again why I thought running a restaurant would be a good idea?" he whispered toward the ceiling. But his mama was, as usual, silent on these matters. And if she'd been looking down on the day he'd had today, he didn't blame her, because there wasn't much to say. Some days, the weight of responsibility was a fucking stone around his neck.

First Rao, one of the line cooks, called in sick with a stomach virus. And then Nicole, one of the waitresses, had gone home with the same thing, followed by Patrick the busboy, Shane the bartender, and Marisol, one of the kitchen staff. Unfortunately, the Saturday night crowd hadn't gotten the memo that half his staff was out sick, and they'd shown up in droves, one rush after another, keeping him hopping from mid-afternoon until they'd ushered the last stragglers out half an hour ago.

He hadn't even done the prep work for the next day's Sunday brunch, which went against every single thing he'd been taught in culinary school and had learned over the past few years running his restaurant, but *fuck it*. He was done.

He pushed himself off the door and up the stairs, imagining Tess waiting for him. Maybe she'd be snuggled up on the couch, the way she'd been when he came home the other night, so he could stretch out behind her and pretend to watch some stupid romantic movie while he really watched *her* watch the movie, instead. Or maybe she'd already be in his bed, which had been *their* bed for the past week, and he could wake her up slowly, his mouth finding that spot on her neck that made her go crazy and his hands roaming up and under one of those sexy nighties that seemed specially designed to make him hard as iron…

Down, boy. Maybe you should spend some time being her dominant, rather than just sexing her up every time you're in the same room.

He rubbed the back of his neck wearily as he trudged down the hall. The past few days had been insanely busy, between hosting private functions, preparing quarterly taxes, getting Nora trained as a waitress, and, in the off-time, helping Matteo renovate his bathroom. And all the while, this stupid voice in the back of his head told him he should be doing more for Tess, but honest to God, he didn't know what. Things between them—the smirks and smiles and smoldering looks, the joy of coming home to her at night, the fucking combustible heat of them in bed together—was beyond his wildest dreams. But he couldn't shake the feeling that it wasn't enough.

Shouldn't he be making more official rules or spanking her on the regular? Shouldn't he be investing in floggers or chains or some shit? Shouldn't he know what the fuck he was doing? How long until she got bored with him? How long until he wasn't enough? How long until she left him for a real dom? The stupid voice just wouldn't shut up. And thinking about it made him more tired than ever, but something had to be done.

So maybe he'd wake her and they'd talk, and *then* they'd move on to the other stuff.

He opened his apartment door... and stopped short.

Damn it. He'd forgotten Nora would be here tonight.

His brown leather sofa was festooned with clothing in various shades of sparkly pink and black. The pounding bass wasn't coming from his neighbor's apartment, but from the cheesy dance music playing on his own speakers. And the source of the laughter that could be heard all the way downstairs wasn't a party full of people, but one tiny blonde dynamo, currently curled up on the floor and shrieking with mirth, her attention centered on the makeshift "stage" of his sturdy wood coffee table.

And he couldn't blame her.

"Baby, I don't need dollar bills to have fun toniiiight..." Tess sang... screeched, yelled... into a plastic hairbrush. Her spectacular ass, hugged by the tiniest scrap of black shorts he'd ever seen, shimmied to the beat of the music, and her long auburn ponytail swayed back and forth.

Jesus.

Some unknown emotion welled up in his stomach, pushing away his shitty mood and lifting the weight from his shoulders. Before he could identify it, Nora had jumped up from the floor in her pink patterned pajamas and bare feet, and joined Tess on the table for the chorus, throwing her wild blonde hair around in a way that would've made any 90s headbanger jealous.

"I love cheap thrills!" the girls screamed into the single hairbrush.

Tess tossed the brush onto the sofa and grabbed both of Nora's hands, swaying them back and forth together in some kind of push-pull dance, giggling madly. Tony leaned against the doorframe to watch the show.

It was the kind of shit his mother used to do with Dom and Matt and him when they were little… with better music, of course, since his mom had been a Stones fan. It was innocent and joyful and it made his chest tight for a whole bunch of reasons he didn't want to think about, but one thing he knew for sure—he wanted this beauty, this goodness in his life. And he'd do whatever he had to do to make sure she started to see herself the way he saw her.

He thought back to her confession the other night and shook his head. She'd had a truly shitty childhood, and she'd been forced to make some tough decisions. But how the hell could she doubt for a minute that she was a good person?

When the music finally ended a few minutes later, Tess pumped her fist in the air in victory, and both girls bowed to an imaginary audience.

Then Tony clapped…

And both girls whirled around, screeching.

He'd thought the show was cute, but their outraged embarrassment was even cuter.

"Tony!" Tess yelled, jumping down from the table. "What time is it? I didn't think you'd be home until…"

"Midnight?" he asked, amused. "It's a little after that now."

"Crap! Really?" she asked, frantically collecting the discarded black and pink clothing from the sofa and stuffing it in a cardboard box, while Nora walked over to turn off the stereo. "Nora was going to try out for the dance team, so I got out my old dance costumes and we put on some music so I could help her practice and I guess I lost track of…"

"Hey, chill," Tony told her, walking over to where she stood by the table, looking adorably flustered. He grabbed her face in his hands and bent down to kiss her softly.

Mmm. Cherry lip gloss.

"You're not mad?" she asked, wrapping her arms around his waist and peeking up at him hesitantly.

"Babe. Why would I be mad?" he asked, shaking his head.

"I figured you'd be tired, and I wanted to have everything cleaned up and settled down before you got here…"

"Yeah, I was tired. *Am* tired, I guess," he amended, although the worst of his fatigue had somehow fled. "But this is your place, too. And I love to see you having fun."

Her brown eyes softened and she bit her lip. "Yeah?"

"Yeah," he told her, bending his head for another taste of cherry.

"Why, hello, Tony!" Nora said pointedly from behind them.

Tess broke the kiss, but didn't move away.

"Why hello, Nora," he told her, still looking at Tess.

"Oh, don't mind *me*," Nora told him. "I can totally handle your half of the conversation, too. 'Hey, Nora, my favoritest employee *ever* and all-around *awesome person*! It's so nice to see you tonight!' Why, thanks for having me, Tony! 'Gee, anytime, Nora! I appreciate that you're such a good influence on Tess, playing her all the cool new songs so she can practice her awesome moves.' Why, you're welcome, Tony! No problem at all."

Tess, who had started giggling at "favoritest employee," absolutely cracked up at "awesome moves."

Tony kissed her laughing mouth one last time before winking at her and turning to her sister, who was standing with her hands on her hips, smiling at them.

"Snazzy jammies, Nor. Are those cartoon characters?"

Nora rolled her eyes and flopped down on the sofa with abandon. "I happen to *enjoy* Dora the Explorer," she told him. "We both like adventure. She's an underappreciated heroine in many ways."

"I'll take your word for it. If I'd known you had this much energy, I would've called you to come work tonight," he told her. Then turning to Tess, he explained, "Rao, Nicki, Pat, Shane, and Mari all called in. Stomach bug."

Tess's eyes widened, and he watched her shift from soft,

tentative, and laughing, to competent, clear-eyed, take-charge manager, as though a switch had flipped in her mind.

Shit, that was hot.

"Crap! You were short-staffed? And on a Saturday night? Why didn't you call me? I would've gone in!" she admonished.

"Yep, I know you would, babe. But I wanted you to have the night off. And it's a good thing I didn't call. I forgot Nora the Explorer was coming over."

"Hey!" Nora protested loudly from the couch. "*Nora the Explorer*? No way! That's the worst name ever."

"Dude, you practically wrapped that name in a bow and gave it to me as a present," he told her, shaking his head with mock regret. "No take-backsies."

He returned his attention to the woman in his arms and continued, "I forgot Nora would be here, but I wanted you to have some downtime. Things will only be getting crazier for the next few months, and you need to rest up."

Tess shook her head in exasperation, but then rose on her tiptoes to give him a soft, searching kiss, a thank you. And he realized he'd do the whole awful night over and over again, just to have her look at him the way she was right now. Like he was fucking magical.

And then her brain swung back to the practical once more.

"I'll call Mark and Carolyn in the morning, see if they can fill in. Plus, we could call Alice. She's not supposed to start for a few weeks, but she's already filled out her paperwork, so maybe she can come in…"

Tony bent his head and cut off her words with a kiss. Partly because she was sexy as hell in her tank top and microscopic shorts. Partly because her calm, efficient tone gave him some childish need to ruffle her feathers. And partly because she was *his* and he fucking *could.*

"Tony!" she protested a moment later. "I was just trying to…"

He kissed her again. He ignored Nora, giggling on the couch, and for just a moment, blocked out all the problems that awaited them at the restaurant in the morning and all the niggling doubts about his ability to be enough for her, and did what came naturally. He focused on nothing but kissing her until she stopped protesting, wrapped her arms around his neck, and kissed him back.

Long moments later, he finally lifted his head to find her looking adorably confused.

"I think it's time for bed, babe."

She nodded like someone in a trance, and it made him chuckle.

"Got plans tomorrow, favoritest employee ever?" he asked Nora.

Nora looked back and forth between him and Tess and grinned hugely. "If that's your way of asking me to come in and help out tomorrow, I'm down. Better get some sleep. 'Night, guys." She picked herself off the sofa and walked off towards the spare room down the hall.

"I really like that kid," Tony told Tess.

Tess smiled. "Me too," she said softly. "And she's probably right. It'll be a busy day tomorrow and you're already tired. We should probably get some sleep."

Tony pretended to think about it, then nodded. "We should, baby, and we will. But first…"

He spun her around so that her back was pressed up against his front, and rested his hands lightly on her hips. He nipped lightly at her earlobe, loving the way she instinctively pressed herself back against him.

"I've heard a rumor that you have some *awesome moves*," he breathed in her ear, as he directed her towards their bedroom. "And I think I'm gonna need to see them for myself."

Tony unlocked the alley door and let himself into *Cara*, juggling his travel mug and the hanger that held the clean uniform he'd change into once the restaurant opened. The chill of the predawn October air had managed to sink into his bones just on the short walk from the car, and he was so fucking tired it wasn't even funny.

Not that he was complaining, not *really*. Not at *all*. Because, yeah, yesterday had sucked. And yeah, the thought of doing it all again today, plus handling the catering for three separate events tonight, was enough to make a man's balls shrivel. And yeah, he was still worried about all the shit he should be doing for Tess that he wasn't capable of doing. And yeah, maybe it would've been a little easier if he'd had a couple more hours of sleep.

But then he wouldn't have had last night with Tessa, and *that* was unthinkable.

He'd told her he wanted to see her dance. And his girl, his honest-to-God fantasy come to life, hadn't hesitated before she'd whispered, "Should I get my costumes?"

And that was it. Game over for him forever. Because no other sexual experience would ever rival the utter perfection of seeing her ass peeking out from beneath a sparkly dance skirt as she crouched chest-down on their bed and presented herself to him for a spanking. Her skin had been so fucking smooth, so perfect, so warm beneath his hand after he'd…

Shit.

He shifted the hanger to his other hand so that he could adjust himself. Today was gonna be long enough without walking around with a hard-on for the next eighteen hours.

He stomped to his office and hung up his clothes, then made his way back to the kitchen. His *occupied* kitchen.

"Morning, boss," John sang as he rolled out dough on the counter. "You're in early! Isn't it beautiful out there today? Don't you just love autumn?"

Tony sipped his coffee and contemplated the other man with

a scowl. The sun hadn't risen, but the kitchen already smelled deliciously of vanilla and butter from the trays of cooling pastries, and silver bowls lined up along one counter held various fillings and sauces. Logically, Tony knew John was used to his early-bird productivity—he did the baking for *Cara* and for his own catering business, and had usually cleaned up and cleared out long before the rest of the staff arrived, leaving cupcakes and other tasty treats for them like a benevolent pastry fairy. For this reason and many others, he had quickly become one of Tony's favorite people.

But that ended now. People who functioned before dawn were an abomination.

"Rough night, huh?" John joked, watching him with wide blue eyes.

Tony knew that John was slightly older than he was, somewhere around thirty, but those eyes, along with his always-perfectly-styled wavy brown hair made him look much younger and more innocent, like an overgrown angel. Until he opened his sarcastic mouth.

"Ah, I see," John said, nodding sagely. "Looks like Tessie left you in a fuck-coma. Well, when you're ready to emerge, blink twice."

Tony shook his head and headed around the counter to the station beside John's, pulling his apron off its peg as he passed.

"Anyone ever tell you you're really fucking annoying this early in the morning?" he grumbled.

John snickered. "Um, that would be Paul. Every single morning. Which is one of the reasons he was thrilled when I took this job and had to come in early. He says I *look* at him too loudly, like he can hear all the thoughts in my brain, and it wakes him up." He shrugged.

Tony had new sympathy for Paul. "Never good to drive your boyfriend crazy first thing in the morning," he told John. He went to the refrigerator and took out a tray of washed produce, ready to be chopped. "Gotta let him ease into the day."

John hmphed. "Is that what's wrong with you this morning? Tessa driving you crazy?"

Tony let the tray fall on the counter with a clatter and turned to look at the other man. "Excuse me?"

John shrugged and kept his eyes on the pastry dough he was turning on the counter. "You're in a surly mood. I wondered if there was trouble in paradise, and maybe I could help. If you wanna talk about it, I can listen. That's all."

Tony bit back his impatience. *Surly*. Who the fuck even used the word *surly*? He wasn't surly. And he most definitely didn't want to talk about anything, that was for damn sure. He wasn't some Neanderthal who pretended he didn't *have* feelings… but he'd be damned if he'd stand around *talking* about them. Plus, talking about his feelings made shit more real.

Still, he knew John meant well. Mostly.

"I'm just tired. And yeah, Tess and I got into it a little bit this morning, but it was no big deal," Tony said, giving John part of the story. "Bunch of people called in sick with a stomach bug yesterday, and Tess is all hyped up and ready to problem-solve." He snorted and shook his head at the memory. She was so fucking cute. "I told her there was nothing she could do at this hour, and I didn't want her to see her here until 10:30 at the earliest. She's bringing Nora."

John looked at him, eyes wide with alarm. "And what did she say about that?"

"Nothing. I mean, she wasn't happy. Tried to explain that she could help with the prep. Like I really need help chopping veggies when she already works a million hours a week." He rolled his eyes and grabbed one of his chef's knives, demonstrating how he made short work of dicing a bell pepper. "But I told her *no*, and she went back to bed. No big deal." Except that the way she'd flipped her hair and sashayed back to their room had provided him with another glorious visual.

"No big deal," John echoed. "You know that Tess is a steam roller, right? Couple weeks ago, Rao and Mark were talking shit and things got heated. Tess stepped in and threatened to fire both their asses. Had this former-Army sergeant and the toughest street kid I've ever met ready to cry without even raising her voice. But with you, she just gave in. And it's no big deal?"

Tony shrugged again. "Well, yeah." Tess had always deferred to him on the rare occasions when he laid down the law like that. It was a given.

John nodded slowly, as though seeing something Tony didn't.

"So can we drop it now? How's Paul?"

"He's great. We're going mountain biking later," John said, waving a hand dismissively at Tony's attempt to change the subject. After a moment's pause, he continued, "You know, I've only known Tess for a few months now, but I've legit never seen her as happy as she's been the past couple of weeks. I think you're good for her. Your relationship is good for her."

Tony grunted noncommittally. John had no clue. Sure, things were great now, but what would happen when she realized she needed a real dom?

"I think you've got something special," John continued, undeterred by Tony's lack of enthusiasm. "Like with Heidi and Dom, and Hillary and Matteo."

Tony huffed out an annoyed breath. "Not quite."

"No, seriously," John said. "It's *just* like that."

"Dude, I know you mean well, but…"

"You're making *her* happy, she's making *you* happy…"

"Man, I don't wanna talk about this. Butt *out*."

"I'm just saying it's a good thing!" John said, holding up his hands in mock innocence. "She's *happy!*"

"Yeah, she's happy for now!" Tony finally exploded, tossing

the knife down on the counter with a clatter. "But who knows how long that will last?"

John turned to him, calmly wiping his hands on the kitchen towel at his waist, completely unperturbed, as though he'd been expecting this outburst. "What makes you think it won't last *forever?*" he asked gently.

Fuck. Exactly what Tony was trying to *avoid* thinking about this morning. Precisely the conversation he *didn't* want to have.

"Tess has… She wants…" He blew out a frustrated breath. "I'm not sure I can give Tess everything she needs, okay?"

John leaned a hip on the counter. "Like, you don't love her? You don't want a long-term relationship?"

"No! *Christ*, no. Of course I want long-term with her. It's just that she has other things she needs," he said lamely. "Drop it. *Please.*"

John nodded and turned back to his dough, leaving Tony alone with his diced veggies and his crappy thoughts.

But not for long.

"You know, Tess and I have a lot in common," John said hesitantly.

"Mmhmm," Tony agreed. "I've heard you have an hour-long conversation about Real Housewives of Wherethefuckever. It was scarring."

"Not that, asshole," John said, shaking his head.

Tony turned and glared at him, one eyebrow raised.

"Ah, I meant, not that, *boss,*" John amended. "Sorry."

Tony nodded. Damn straight. He returned his attention to his chopping.

"I mean, certain *other* things in common. Um, *relationship* things."

"Like you're both into guys?" Tony asked, looking up in surprise. "This isn't news, buddy." Not that John had ever hidden his sexual orientation, but John's boyfriend Paul was best friends with Heidi, and that's how Tony and John had first met, so it was hardly a secret.

John nodded. "But beyond that. We're both, um… submissives." He said the last word in a rush and his face turned beet red.

Tony turned to look at him. "Yeah. I know."

"You do? Does it freak you out?" John asked softly.

Tony shook his head firmly. "Nah. Makes me think I'm the only guy in Boston who's *not* into this stuff, though."

"You're not?" John's face fell. "*Oh*. Oh, that *could* be a problem."

Tony snorted, even as the confirmation made his gut burn. "No shit, Sherlock. Geez, this was fucking helpful. Can sharing time be over now?"

John contemplated him with a frown. "Are you *sure* you're not into it? Not even a little?"

Tony set down the knife and stared at the other man, crossing his arms over his chest. Was he really gonna talk about this?

Fuck him. Apparently he was.

He sighed. "Spanking her ass in bed is about the hottest thing I've ever done or seen, okay? But the rest? Making up rules, doling out punishments, being that stern, hard-assed guy?" He blew out a breath and thought of his beautiful Tess, of her soft brown eyes and her scars, both visible and invisible. "She's had enough people in her life who hurt her and punished her and told her she wasn't good enough. If I ever made her feel that way, if I made her sad, what would that say about me?"

John nodded. "Well, right. I mean, if you broke her heart, I would kick your ass," John told him.

Tony shot him a look, but John stared back defiantly. Tony nodded. *Fair enough.*

"But then you see my problem, dude. How do I punish her, make her feel bad… when I mostly want to keep her safe and happy every minute of the day?" Tony shook his head glumly.

"Not gonna work. And I, uh…" Shit. How could he talk about this without being too personal? "I've heard that some people who like this stuff need to be spanked regularly. Like, if they don't, they miss it. And fun, little sexy spankings aren't enough. They need to be more… real."

John nodded. "Yeah, that's true. For some of us, the spankings help us connect with our emotions in a way we can't otherwise. Brings things to the surface. It's a pain that we can let ourselves feel. And it feels good to give up control to someone who deserves it. Cathartic, you know?"

"Kinda like pounding the hell out of a bag at the gym?" Tony guessed.

John smiled. "Probably. I'll take your word for it." He winked and Tony smirked. Then John continued, "But you know, there doesn't necessarily have to be a punishment involved if you don't want there to be."

"What?" Wasn't that the whole point?

John ran a hand through his perfect brown hair and tried to explain. "You said you like spanking her in bed, right? Well, why not give her a stress-relief spanking when she needs it? When you see her getting agitated, when you see that she's spiraling, spank her. Not as punishment, and not because she broke a rule, but because she needs it. And not a fun little spank. A hard one, one that she can really feel, one that goes on for a while. Cathartic, like I said."

A serious spanking that wasn't about discipline so much as keeping her grounded? Something he could give her that would help her deal with shit? Keep her happy?

"Yeah, okay. I could do that." His mind flashed back to his palm slapping her rosy cheeks the night before, and he felt a flush work over his face. "I could *definitely* do that."

John smiled. "Well, there you go, then!"

Uh, not quite. Tony took a deep breath and spoke the words that had been rattling around his brain for weeks.

"But how long until she gets tired of the half-assed thing?"

John looked at him skeptically. "Half-assed?"

"No rules, no punishments. No whips and chains and floggers. I'm not that guy, John. For Tess, I almost want to try to be, but I can't. I spent *months* with Val trying to be someone I'm not, and I can't go back to that. Not even for Tess." He raked his fingers through his hair and paced the kitchen in agitation. "I'm not a dominant. Not really. I *like* when she's sassy. I *love* watching her take charge of the restaurant and kick ass. That story about her making Mark and Rao cry? Hot as fucking hell."

John snickered. "Yeah. Objectively speaking, it kinda was."

Tony snorted. Jesus, this guy.

"But, Tony, you've got a whacked idea of what this stuff is all about. There's no one definition of what this dynamic means, and no right or wrong way to do it. It's whatever you want it to be and whatever Tess needs it to be. You just need to talk to her and figure out what that is."

John was looking at him earnestly, and Tony wanted to believe what he was saying, but it sounded a little too good to be true.

"I appreciate you trying, man," Tony said, resuming his place at his station. "Let's drop it for now and we'll see how it goes, okay?" He grabbed an enormous metal bowl and tossed in all his chopped vegetables, along with some oil and seasoning in preparation for roasting, effectively ending the conversation.

If only he could shut his thoughts off as easily.

Out of the corner of his eye, he saw John nod and turn his attention to his own work, placing dough in the refrigerator to chill, and taking cooled pastries off the rack to fill.

"Hey, boss? Which is better, chocolate filling or vanilla?"

Tony turned to look at the half-dozen bowls in front of John. "Huh?"

"Which is better, vanilla crème anglaise or chocolate mousse? Or strawberry compote? Or crème caramel? Chopped apples and brandy? Cinnamon cayenne pecans? Which one?" John asked, pointing to each silver bowl in turn.

He asked this like it was a normal question, but Tony couldn't remember John ever asking his opinion in the past. Like, *ever*.

"Do you mean for the catered banquet tonight? Or for brunch? Or dinner? Don't you always do, you know, a variety?" Tony asked in confusion.

"Yeah, but I'm asking which is *best*," John said.

Tony shook his head. "You mean, in my *opinion*? I like caramel, but they're all good. Chocolate mousse is popular, I think."

"Yes, but which is *right*, Tony? Which is the real filling, the *correct* filling?" John pressed.

"Correct? Correct for *what*? Dude, what the hell are you talking about?" Tony asked.

"I'm talking about D/s, Tony. And you just illustrated my point. There's no *one* right flavor for everyone."

Tony blinked. Then blinked again. Well, *shit*.

"A dominant's job is really hard," John said, his eyes on his work as he filled a pastry bag with the decadent chocolate mousse. "You have to focus on your sub, learn to read her needs, know when to comfort and when to push, so you can help her be happy and fulfilled. You can't seriously imagine there's a one-size-fits-all solution to that, right? 'Cause if there's not a one-size solution for something as simple as *dessert*, man, how can there be one size for relationships?"

Tony swung his gaze back to his work station, and stared hard at the empty counter. Was it really that easy? Hope surged in his gut, seized his chest, made it hard to breathe.

"The kink aspect alone!" John continued as he filled puff pastries, unaware of the revelations Tony was having. "The spectrum would astound you. Whips and chains don't work for you?

Well, me neither. Your two most effective implements are attached to your *wrists*."

John squirmed uncomfortably, as if remembering something.

Tony squirmed too, for a different reason. "Dude, you don't need to share."

"Same goes with the rules," John continued, oblivious to Tony's discomfort. "Most of the time, doms establish certain standards of behavior that are usually in the sub's best interest. You're only into safety rules? Great. You don't mind her sassing you? Well, *lucky Tess*, because some of us get punished *repeatedly* for failing to learn *that* one, and I mean with the fucking *paddle*, which is no joke."

"Jesus, John! Enough!" The mental pictures Tony was getting of his friends could never truly be bleached away.

John turned his head to look at Tony and sighed. "Fine, *fine*. Essentially, I'm saying there's no Dominant Club that's gonna revoke your membership for not doing things a certain way. And no dominant worth his salt would *join* one, if there were such a thing. It's all about you and your girl. You trust her to follow your lead, she trusts you to lead her, and no one else gets a damn vote. You get me, Sparky?"

Tony snorted. "Yeah. I get you. I also totally get how you keep getting punished for sass. Watch it," he warned, pointing a finger at John sternly.

John nodded quickly. "Not a real dom, my ass," he muttered under his breath. In a louder voice, he said, "You're taking care of her, Tony. You're worrying about what she needs. You're letting her be who she needs to be, and supporting her the whole way. *That* is what a dominant does. And Tess recognizes it. A woman as strong as Tess wouldn't submit to you if she didn't."

Relief flooded him, making him fucking lightheaded and filled with new determination.

"Thank you, John," he said sincerely. "Really."

John smiled. "You're welcome, Tony. *Really*."

"But, John?" Tony added, with just a touch of menace in his voice. "If you ever tell *anyone* the specifics of what we discussed? I'll kill you."

John rolled his eyes. "You totally *killed* the happy moment we were just sharing! Did you think I was going to take out a billboard and announce it to the world?"

If Tony had thought that, he wouldn't have shared in the first place. But it was worth ensuring.

"Not kidding, John." He folded his arms across his chest.

John huffed. "Bite me, Tony."

"*Jesus*. You really *don't* learn." Tony shook his head.

"Well then it's just as well you're not my dom," John told him smugly. "You're *Tessa's*."

"That's right," Tony agreed, grinning hugely as he felt the truth of the statement flow through him. "I am."

Chapter 7

Tessa cranked up the music as she drove to work, bopping along with the windows rolled down. It was normally chilly in Boston this time of year, but fall was unpredictable. Some days would be chilly and brisk, and others sunny and warm. Today was a warmer day than usual as the sun shone. Her mind wandered as she remembered what Tony had done the night before.

All day, *all day long*, at *Cara*, he'd flirted with her. Frankly, she didn't know what had gotten into him. He locked the door to her office during lunch, and drew her onto his lap for a make-out session, until a knock sounded on the door. She had Tony go answer it while she frantically threw a plastic container of paperclips on the floor, just so she could pretend to be stooped over and pick them up, avoiding looking John in the eye when he asked about the amount of pastries needed for the event they were hosting that evening. Nora needed a ride in the afternoon, so Tony had tagged along with her, joking around with Nora as they picked up shakes at a drive-thru. When Tessa had arrived back at *Cara*, she teased him, and before she'd entered the restaurant, he'd delivered a teasing, but pointed swat on her ass, causing her to spin around and stare at him, wide-eyed. He'd merely shrugged. "Act the part of a brat, get treated like one," he said. It didn't help that they were in such good company at *Cara*. Hillary, Heidi, or John would think nothing of a smack being delivered as she entered the restaurant.

Or would they? She wondered how much their friends picked up on things. They'd given up keeping their relationship secret. Tony insisted there was no need. But still, they had to maintain the bare minimum requirement of professionalism.

By the time he'd gotten her home that evening, she was primed, and they had a fun night together, complete with him blindfolding her and making her come until she screamed his name. She sighed. It had been delightful.

With a frown, she realized she'd been so caught up in her memories of the evening's festivities with Tony, that she'd completely missed her turn. She'd bypassed the intersection where *Cara* was, and instead had arrived in an unfamiliar place. It was surprisingly more run-down than where she'd usually gone. Several houses on one side of the street looked dilapidated. One had a car in the driveway with flat tires and an overgrown lawn. Several had boarded-up windows, and to her right, a passel of teen-aged boys was passing around something that looked like a joint.

Where the hell was she?

She drove down one street, certain that if she took a turn somewhere, she'd be able to find her way back to the main intersection that would take her to *Cara*. But the further she drove, the more lost she became. Finally, huffing out a breath as she glanced at the time on her dash, she pulled to the side of the road. She took out her cell phone, enabling GPS and punching in the address for *Cara*, when something immediately outside her window made her freeze. Blonde hair that hung about her shoulders in waves. An hour-glass figure in a skin-tight skirt and midriff top.

The profile and view from where she sat looked *exactly* like her mother.

Tessa's palms grew sweaty, as she blinked. Her mother was older now, her hair cut shorter, and clothes hung limply on her instead of hugging her curves. This *couldn't* be her mother. And as the woman turned to Tessa, she caught her eye. She was a complete stranger. Tessa had never seen the woman in her life. But as she marched to Tessa's car with purposeful strides, Tessa began to panic. Before the woman could reach her window and asked for whatever it was she needed—a light, a drive, or maybe some money—Tessa was gone She'd floored it.

She fiddled with the GPS until she found her way back to *Cara*, but the situation was strangely unsettling, like she'd somehow accidentally ended up in a sort of weird time warp. Her hands shook as she removed the keys from her ignition. Shutting the car door, she removed her bag and stepped outside.

Tony was just exiting the back door with a large trash bag and some boxes in his hands.

"Hey, beautiful," he crooned, giving her a chin lift.

"Hey," she responded. She needed to get inside.

It wasn't the only thing she needed.

God, she needed a *spanking*. It'd been a few days since she'd gone over Tony's lap, and she hadn't been to The Club in weeks. Her hands shook. But she put on a brave face, accustomed to ignoring her needs. She didn't want Tony to see that she was about to lose her shit because she got lost and saw someone who reminded her of her mom. Seriously, who *did* that?

So while she blew past Tony, bent on keeping her head in the game, she ignored him. He followed behind her, but she didn't want him to see her hands shaking, or hear her voice quavering if she spoke. A minute later, she heard the heavy door to *Cara* close, and Tony was talking to some of his employees in the kitchen. Making a beeline to her office, she turned to shut the door behind her, but Tony was already there.

"Hey! Whoa, babe, you're like a bat outta hell. What's going on?" he asked, as he held the doorknob, followed her in, and shut it gently.

Tessa shrugged. "Nothing. Just having a weird morning."

He took her by the hand and pulled her into him. The hug felt nice. But it wasn't what she needed.

How could she tell him she was creeped out by the odd accidental spin down an unknown street? How could she tell this sweet, loving guy that what she needed from him wasn't a hug, or a similar gentle gesture, but a long session over his lap? It wasn't necessarily the pain of a spanking, but submitting to him—a strong, capable, loving guy—that made the stress melt away. It was the buzz she got from feeling his strength, and the hormonal release and erotic jolt from a good spanking.

She stiffened as he hugged her, then gently pried his hands off of her and walked to her desk.

"Gotta get shit done, Tony," she finally said. He frowned.

"Tess, why are you getting all weird on me?"

"I'm not getting *weird on you*," she responded, feeling rising anger. What the *hell?* "Don't you have ravioli to cut or something?" She pulled out her ledger. It was time to do some serious accounting. They were in good shape, but needed to stay that way. She leaned under the table and grabbed a can of Diet Coke, and when she sat back up again, she jumped. The ledger had been snatched up, sitting in Tony's lap, while he sat in the chair across from her with his arms across his chest.

She swallowed. His eyes narrowed on her, his jaw set, his large arms crossed uncompromisingly. She wasn't getting away with the old "tell him everything's fine" line. So much for thinking Tony wasn't really dom material.

"What?" she said. She could *feel* her lips turning down in a scowl. "And give me my damn ledger."

"No."

"*No?*"

He leaned down across the table, both hands planted firmly on her desk. "*No.* And I'm bigger and stronger, so I get my way. Woman. *Spill.*"

"It's nothing," she said. "For God's sake, Tony, give me my goddamned ledger."

He continued to gaze at her before he replied. "Now I see the appeal of the whole spanking thing."

She swallowed. "You want to spank me?"

He shrugged. "Do you need a spanking?"

She slumped in her seat and buried her face in her hands. "Yes. *Yes.* God, I need a spanking so bad." Her voice shook a little as she spoke. "I was on my way into work and I was… sort of reliving everything we did last night. I took a wrong turn and got lost, and it was fine because I just pulled it up on my GPS. It was only a few turns in the wrong direction. But I saw this woman, Tony…" She lifted her face from her hands and looked at him. He still looked stern, but now placid, compassionate even. "I saw this woman who looked just like my mother. She was… younger. It couldn't have been her. But she looked just like my mom did years ago, and it freaked me out. It was like… seeing a ghost. A not very nice ghost."

She closed her eyes. She could still feel the dread pooling in her stomach as she walked up the stairs to her home, wondering if today she'd be alone, or with her normal mom, or with the mom who would hurt her.

She felt Tony grasping her hand, and opened her eyes.

"Baby," he said gently. "Have you thought about going to see someone?"

Tessa sat up, the moment gone, as she yanked her hand back from him. "Like a *shrink? Geez.* Way to kill a moment."

His eyes grew stern. "Like a therapist, Tess. And no need for you to get all mad at me for suggesting it."

She glared at him. "You think I'm damaged goods. Just like

all the other guys I dated, you think I'm some sort of freak. Too fucked up to handle."

"*No.*"

"You do!" she said, rising to her feet, conscious enough of the fact that their employees were on the other side of her office door, so she kept her voice to a low hiss. "Don't even lie to me. Just tell me the truth. You think I'm crazy!"

He crossed the length between his chair and her desk in two long strides, grabbing her by the wrist and pulling her over to where he was. He sat, tugging her onto his lap as she pushed against him.

"You sit here like a good girl and listen to me."

Or what? Her mind asked. *You'll spank me?*

Would he? Oh, how she wanted him to.

She pushed back against him. "And what if I say no?" she hissed. "What if I don't *want* to listen to you?"

She yelped as he twisted her over his lap and spanked her, one hard smack she felt straight through the thin fabric of her skirt. It shocked her, and she fell silent.

"You will listen to me because I'm the guy who cares about you," he said hotly. "You will listen to me because you need to talk, and you also need to listen. And you will listen to me because I'm not letting you off my lap until you do, and I don't care what you try, I'm bigger than you and you won't get away."

She sat meekly on his lap. She was beginning to feel a bit more relaxed. It felt nice sitting on his lap. He was a big guy, and feeling him all around her made her feel like she was special to him.

"Are you going to be a good girl?" he asked.

She nodded.

"Good. Now listen up. First, I'm suggesting you go to a therapist, yes. Not because you're crazy, but because you're hurt. Wounded. And a good therapist merely gives you the tools to help you fix what's broken, and move on with your life."

"That's what everyone says," she said, feeling her anger rising again.

"I don't care what everyone says," he said. "*I* went to a therapist when my parents died, and it was the best thing I ever did."

She looked at him in surprise, her voice soft when she spoke. "You did?"

His eyes met hers squarely while his hands flexed around her. "I did. Not because I was crazy, Tess. Because I didn't have the tools I needed to sort through what I was experiencing, and I wanted to go to someone who knew better. And it helped."

She spoke quietly. "It did?"

He nodded. "Yup."

She'd been to therapists before, and knew the potential for helping her was there. It was the suggestion from *him* that she go that was pissing her off.

"Just something to think about. No making decisions today. Just think about whether or not it will help. Now come here, baby." Gently, he pushed her head down on his chest. "Hold my hand."

She held his hand, her head on his chest, and they sat quietly, not speaking for a while. Gradually, her pent-up emotions began to seep out of her. She felt his heartbeat under her chin.

"See? I'm happy to give you a spanking if you need it. You know that. But I want you to be able to come to me and talk to me first. I know spanking over things like that works for some people, but not us. You get me?"

She nodded. "I do," she whispered.

"Now, tell me. *Do* you need me to spank you?"

She swallowed. "I do. Please. But we can't here…"

He pushed her off his lap and stood to standing. "Right. You and I are taking a quick lunch break."

"But I just got here!"

"…and we'll swing by our place, grab sandwiches, then come back," he continued, as if she didn't just interrupt him.

Had he just said *our* place?

"I have work to do!"

"And unless you want me to do something else, like... I dunno, send you to bed early or something, you'll move your ass *now.*"

She was staring at him incredulously.

"You're crazy," she whispered. "I can't just—leave work, and—"

He nodded soberly, arms across his chest. "Right. Maybe you should ask your boss first. Oh. Wait." He leaned in and his voice dropped. "I *am* your boss. Now unless you want me to spank you *here* where we are very likely to be overheard..."

"No!" She was grabbing her bag and moving toward the door. "Okay, okay, I got it!"

His eyes narrowed at her as he watched her scurry to the door, but his lips twitched.

"Geeez," she muttered under her breath, but still, her heart was soaring. He wouldn't punish her, and she was *okay* with that. He was going to take control of the situation, and *that* was what she needed most.

But as she pushed the door of her office open, and Tony followed behind her, her cell phone rang.

On auto-pilot, she answered.

She heard a strangled cry. Tess frowned, listening harder, as her pulse spiked and her palms grew sweaty.

"Tess!"

"Nora? Nora!" The other line clicked off.

She spun around to look at Tony. He was frowning, as he reached for her phone, and redialed.

"Nothing. Voice mail. Where would she be?"

"My mom's," Tess said. "She told me she was going to swing by there after school to get some books before she came into work."

He was already instructing his employees with what they

needed to do in his absence, as he marched to the door to the parking lot, with Tessa trotting to keep up with him.

Later, she would think to herself that it was a damn good thing Tony *didn't* spank her when she acted out. If that was part of their arrangement, the way she handled him taking over the car situation when they got to the parking lot would've earned her one helluva spanking.

He'd insisted on driving.

"You mean to tell me Nora called you, crying, is likely with your very unpredictable mother and her asshole, drug-addict boyfriend, and you think I'm going to let you just drive on over there? And furthermore, you think I'd let you drive upset like this? Get in the passenger seat of my car, *now.*"

She ignored him. She wanted to be the one to drive in *her* car, and she wasn't about to let him railroad her. He wouldn't drive fast enough.

"No way. I'm driving. Come if you want, but I'm handling this myself."

"The hell you are."

And before she knew what was happening, he was practically carrying her kicking and screaming to where the door of his car was already open. He plunked her bodily in the seat, buckled her, and locked the door.

"You'll thank me later," he said. "Now behave yourself and tell me where to go."

"You can go to *hell!*" she screamed, with half a mind to unbuckle herself but she knew even in her half-crazed state that fighting him would delay the necessary speed they needed. The faster they got to Nora the better. So instead she resorted to muttering under her breath and sending him glares and furious vibes.

His jaw clenched. "Stop acting like a brat. The longer you prolong this, the longer it takes us to get to Nora."

He was right, of course. So she complied, reluctantly.

The whole time they drove, she kept dialing Nora's phone, to no avail. As he pulled down the street that led to her house, she felt the familiar twisting of her stomach and the shallow breathing begin. Just getting closer to her house would set her on the edge of an anxiety attack.

"There it is," she said. They pulled up to the side of the road, and Tessa was out of the car before he'd parked. While Tony yelled her name, she ignored him.

The front door opened, and to Tessa's immense relief, Nora came out, clutching books and clothes to her chest, her blonde hair flying out around her wildly. She was crying.

"Oh, God," Tessa said. "Nora!" Nora looked up, startled, dropping all her belongings on the ground. Nora dropped down and tried to gather up her things and then Tony was there, helping her.

"Tell us what's going on, Nora. Now," he said, head still bent down picking up stacks of papers that had fallen out of Nora's bag.

"She went on a rampage. This is the last straw," Nora said with a shaking voice. "After this and what happened last night, I just can't live here anymore."

Tessa felt her heart constrict as she looked to Nora. No telltale signs of abuse. Just tears. "Did she hurt you?" she whispered.

Nora shook her head. "No. She wouldn't. I told her the last time that if she ever laid a hand on me again I'd go to the police." Her sister's eyes met hers with steely determination.

Tessa nodded, and Tony murmured, "Good girl," as he continued to pick things up.

Nora stood, and Tess wrapped her arms around the girl's shoulders.

"Last night, R-Roger said…" Nora's eyes filled with tears. "He said it was time I started paying my way around here."

"What the hell does that mean?" Tony demanded.

Nora shook her head. "I don't know exactly. But I think I can guess. He's been bringing his friends around the house more and more often. They all crash in the living room and get high as kites, and then sit around talking about *scores* and *deals* and *revenge* like they're some kind of mafia kingpins. I thought it was all just stupid talk. That those guys were too stupid to be criminal masterminds, you know?"

Her voice broke as she continued, "But the way they look at me, Tess. And then last night, one of them, the guy they call Chalo, had a gun."

"What?" Tess said, gripping Nora's shoulders tight. "You're okay?"

Nora nodded, her eyes filling with tears. "Yeah. I'm okay. He didn't fire it. He just laid it on the arm of the chair, and then…"

"What?" Tony asked gently, standing with Nora's belongings in his hands.

Nora swallowed. "He told me to kiss him." Nora looked from Tony to Tess and continued, "Like maybe he'd shoot me if I didn't."

"Jesus," Tony whispered, his eyes flashing as he clenched his jaw.

"This other really scary guy, Diego, told him to shut the fuck up and remember they didn't need trouble. They kinda got into it. I ran back to our bedroom and locked the door, and I think they maybe forgot about me."

"And what did *Mom* say?" Tess cried.

"She wasn't home last night. But when she got back this morning, I told her. She said Roger knew what was best for me. She said I needed to stop pretending I was better than her like my…" her voice dropped. "Like my stuck-up bitch of a sister," Nora confessed. "She said she knew I'd been working for you at

Cara. And then she destroyed my stuff, Tess. Smashed my cell phone. Tore my school books. Threw all my clothes—"

Of course her mother would destroy everything that gave Nora hope of ever leaving, of ever having a better life. Tessa's fists clenched with the need to commit violence.

"It's just stuff, baby," Tessa said softly, angrily. "I'll replace all of it. But where is she now? Do you know?"

Nora shook her head. "She knew I was calling you. That's why she broke my phone. And I bet she knew you'd come for me, which is why she left."

"All right," Tony said. "This is what we do. You and Tessa go upstairs and get the rest of the stuff you need. I'll stay here to make sure you're left alone. You've got your phone, Tess?"

Tessa nodded. "I do."

"Be reasonable, Nora. Only what you *need*, okay? We can replace things."

We. Tessa felt her heart constrict.

"Be quick about it. Then we'll bring your stuff to our place."

Our place.

Nora nodded. "Okay," she whispered.

"*Go.*"

Tessa and Nora trotted up the front stairs.

Tessa grabbed grocery bags from the table in the kitchen where empty beer cans and pizza boxes were scattered haphazardly. She raced back to Nora's bedroom, ignoring the living room where more liquor bottles lay tilted on their sides and cigarette butts lay scattered around the tables. She helped Nora shove in some clothes, her school books, and the few things of hers that had meaning before her cell rang. Tony.

"Yeah?"

"Let's go. Quicker, Tess."

"Okay, okay," she said. "Let's go, Nora." She took a deep breath, and said what she'd wanted to say for so long. "You're coming home with me, honey."

Nora was dead asleep in Tony's spare room. Tony had called and made sure everything was situated at *Cara*, explaining that they wouldn't be back in that night. Hillary had called Tessa and asked if everything was okay.

"No, but they will be," she'd said.

"You call me and Matteo if you need anything, babe," Hillary had said. *"Anything."* And Tessa felt her eyes well up with that, because she knew it was true.

Tony had taken the two of them back to his place, *their* place. After they'd determined their mother was not an immediate threat, Tony had insisted Nora get in the car, and he took her to the store to get a new cell phone. Tess wanted to pay for it, but Tony said it was a bonus for his employee. Tess hugged his arm while he helped Nora pick out a new phone and a case. By the time they'd gotten home, it was dinner time. Tess made a salad while Tony grilled chicken and Nora did her homework.

Tess liked that. It felt normal and natural, Nora sitting at the table, one leg tucked under her while she worked math problems in a notebook, while Tessa tossed veggies in a bowl, and Tony hummed along, grilling up chicken. Tony told Nora that she was there to stay, and his tone of voice left no room for argument. Tessa was in complete agreement, of course. Nora *had* to stay. She'd wanted Nora with her safe and sound forever, and now that she was here, Tess wasn't going to let her go.

"We'll have ground rules," Tony had said, pointing the tongs he was using to flip the chicken with at Nora. "We'll want to know where you are, and set up basic rules for living here. Nothing crazy, but we've gotta be on the same page. But we'll talk about that tomorrow." Nora nodded.

Tessa felt her heart warm at that. He hadn't asked her. He hadn't suggested it. There was something protective and sweet about how he was with her baby sister.

And now it was nighttime and Nora was snoring softly in the other room while Tony cleaned up the kitchen. She could not, *would not* ask him for the spanking she needed, even though she needed it now worse than ever.

Tessa's nerves were on edge. Her hands shook. Other people would reach for a drink, or go for a run, or do something normal to relieve the stress. Tess felt her hands shaking as she hiked up the skirt she was wearing. She could feel the scars. Her hands itched to take something sharp and scrape it along the edge of her skin, feeling the pull and tingle of a blade, her heart pounding in fear before the release she would get.

Fuck it. Tony was doing his own thing. Nora was in the other room asleep.

Neither one of them would know. She pushed all thoughts of *this is fucked up* and *tell him before you do something stupid* and *you're beyond this now* right out of her head as she made her way to the bathroom. She couldn't take the tension anymore. She couldn't handle the knot in her stomach and the lump in her throat. The idea of hurting her mother, of *ending* her, was powerful and scary. But as she stared in the medicine cabinet, her razor gleaming in the light, she couldn't do it. Her hands shook as she shut the cabinet.

By the time she went to his room, Tony was sitting in a chair, his ankle across one knee with his arms folded on his chest.

Tess climbed into his bed and sat cross-legged, giving him a sheepish look.

Tony cut right to the chase.

"Someone needs a spanking."

"You do?" she quipped. "Well, I don't usually swing that way, but if you insist, I'll give it a go. Might feel good to get some of this tension out."

His eyes narrowed. "Thin ice, woman. *Thin. Ice.* Level with me. Do you need a spanking?"

Tess swallowed and shrugged. "Maybe."

He raised an eyebrow. "Maybe?"

She cast her eyes down. "Okay. Not maybe. Yes, I need a spanking." She'd been spanked so many times she'd lost count, but it still felt really weird saying it out loud. She squirmed on the bed, not wanting to talk about it. She just wanted him to *do it*.

He stood, crossed the room, and climbed up in bed, pulling her over to him. "C'mere," he said gruffly. "Been a long day, huh?"

She nodded into his chest as he held her. One of his fingers lifted her chin up. Their eyes met.

"You're brave, beautiful. So brave." He leaned down, his lips full and soft, meeting hers. She sighed into his mouth, as one of his hands snaked around the back of her neck and squeezed. The kiss intensified, heating up, as his tongue probed her mouth. One of his hands slowly meandered down the front of her blouse as his thumb gently massaged her nipple. She sighed, as both of his hands lifted and cupped her face. She rose up on her knees, meeting his insistent kiss. And then he pulled away.

"You need a spanking first."

She almost giggled, because he was so cute and she was nervous. He hadn't spanked her very much, but he was good at it. She knelt on the bed, waiting for his instruction, when he reached forward and tugged her over his lap.

"Like this?" she asked.

"Nope," he said, grasping the hem of her skirt and lifting it up, before he pulled her panties down. "Like *this.*"

She gasped as his hand landed firmly on her naked skin. He was quiet for a minute, letting his hand do the talking.

"Nora will hear!" she hissed, but he carried on as if he didn't care for a few more strokes. His hand rested on her bottom.

"Nope. I can still hear her snoring. Good thing your sister's a snorer. Nora the Snorer. I can't wait to christen her with that one tomorrow."

"Tony!" she laughed, wiggling on his lap. "You're not supposed to be cracking jokes while you smack my ass!"

"Oh yeah? Is that in the rule book?" he said, letting loose a particularly sharp swat.

"Yeowch! Ooooh, ow ow ow ow!"

"I think not yelling at your man in the parking lot of your workplace is also in the rule book."

Whack!

"Pretty sure kicking your legs like a little brat in the grocery store whose Daddy won't buy frosted Pop Tarts is also in the rule book."

Whack!

"And I might be new to this? But telling your man how to spank you when you're belly-down over his lap?" *Whack!* "Might not be in *the* rule book." *Whack!* "But it's most definitely in *mine*."

He gave her three more swats. Her whole body was tense, braced for each smack of his hand, but with the next hard crack, she felt the air whoosh out of her. There was always a turning point during a spanking like this. It hurt at first, and she'd wiggle and squirm. But then as it continued, as she grew accustomed to the feel of it, and she was good and warmed up, she'd reach the point where she felt less pain, and a sort of calm would flood her.

"Ahhh," she said, closing her eyes, as his hand paused, squeezing and gently massaging her hot skin. He dipped a finger lower, between her legs, and stroked upward. She gasped. It shouldn't have surprised her how turned on she was, but it did. The immediate feel of his hand spanking her, then pleasuring her, made her squirm. But he only teased her for a minute before his hand was gone again, and she could feel him tense, ready to give her another swat.

Now that she was warmed up, the pain didn't register so much as the warmth and flood of relaxation that tingled through her body. Occasionally, she would wiggle a little, hoping to encourage him. She could feel his erection against her belly, and hear his intake of breath every time she wiggled. With several seconds between swats, he continued, one firm swat at a time.

"Good girl," he said softly. "God this is so fucking hot." His hand paused, massaging her, before he continued again. "Your ass bared to me. The red on your skin. The way you wiggle those hips, and your moans. God."

Swat! Her whole bottom was hot now, fiery and stinging, as he left not a single inch of her untouched. He continued to spank her and her head felt lighter now, like she was almost floating. She was drunk on the erotic release of it all, and her body hummed with need.

"That's enough now," he said in a husky whisper. She felt his large hand on her fiery hot skin, massaging and caressing, before he flicked his finger between her legs, plunging in and pumping. She gasped, grinding against him, her need instantly charged.

"I think you should thank me for your spanking," he said with a chuckle as he released her and she rose to her knees, straddling him. She leaned down and kissed him as he fondled her breast with one hand and pulled her hair firmly with the other.

"Thank you," she whispered. "That was perfect. I didn't know if it would be perfect, but it was."

He chuckled. "Well, you know what they say about practice, baby."

He pushed up, flipping her over as he rolled over on top of her and pinned her down.

"Take 'em off," he growled in her ear. She shimmied out of the panties that hung around her ankles as she pulled off her tank top and skirt. He unbuttoned his jeans. Seconds later, they were bared and he was back, sliding on a condom and holding her in his arms as he entered her. Her hips bucked, the sensation of being full overwhelming her while the burning heat of her spanked ass revved up her need for him. He thrust into her, groaning as he built to climax, and she panted as her own ecstasy consumed her. She came hard, hips rising on the bed beneath his sturdy, husky body, his strong arms pinning her down.

"Baby," he whispered, his forehead on her shoulder. She could see the faintest gleam on his skin from his exertion. She ran a finger along the scruff of his chin, and closed her eyes.

"You know," she whispered softly. "I needed that."

"I know you did," he whispered back.

"I… was tempted to cut myself today, Tony. I made it so far as the bathroom, and when I opened the cabinet door, I couldn't do it."

He sat up so quickly it startled her. His eyes had darkened, his jaw clenched, and for a moment, she was frightened. He so rarely looked like this.

"You listen to me. Are you listening to me?"

She nodded, swallowing.

"Those days are *gone*, Tessa. You don't do that anymore. I'm glad you stopped yourself, but the fact that you even went as far as to go near the razor is not okay with me."

Tears dampened her eyes, but not from sadness. She felt relieved.

He took her chin in his hands and his eyes bore into hers. "I might not be into this whole discipline thing? For *us*, I would much rather spank you to help you relax, or turn you on. I'll help you with what you need, but don't feel totally cool with punishing you for things. You get that?"

She nodded. "I do," she whispered.

"But that is the *one* thing I *will* spank you for. Do you understand me?" His voice was so stern she could hardly look at him.

"Okay," she whispered. "I get it."

He held her eyes for another moment before he nodded, appeased. He was determined to make his point. "I won't like it, Tessa, but if you *ever* do that to yourself, you *will* answer to me. I'm not some other dom. I'm not a club guy, or whatever. But I'm the guy who loves you. And that's where I draw the line."

"I love you, too," she whispered, as he settled back down into bed and she crawled up onto him, one knee hitched up, her head snuggled up under his chin. "Thank you, Tony."

She felt completely at peace, and content with everything. But Tessa had never had normal, and healthy, and good.

She wondered how long it would all last.

Chapter 8

"God, that feels good," Tony groaned, sinking into one of the big brown easy chairs in Matteo's sunny living room and feeling his cramped muscles stretch. He saw Dom and Slay repeat the move, each claiming one end of the sofa adjacent to him and propping their feet on the stone coffee table in the middle of the seating area.

They had been painting and tiling and grouting and installing fixtures all day, four large men crammed into one bathroom—which sounded like the beginning of some really awful porn or the setup for a truly hilarious joke, if Tony hadn't been too exhausted to think up a punch line.

Matteo retrieved four bottles of Sam Adams, Tony's favorite beer, from his fridge and kicked the door closed.

"Whose idea was it to build this place with a bathroom that's bigger than my first apartment?" Slay grumbled.

"Better question: who the hell decided that the entire bottom half of the walls of said bathroom needed to be covered in those little white tiles?" Dom asked. He lifted one hand to massage his shoulder, but his eyes were twinkling.

"Dude, that's not even a question," Tony scoffed.

"Hillary!" all three men said in unison.

Slay snorted. "Gotta keep the little woman happy, eh Matt?" he joked.

Matteo rolled his eyes. "For your information, it's called *subway tile*, dipshit," he said, as he popped the tops off the beers and brought them out to the living room. He passed them out, then sank into the easy chair opposite Tony. "It's a clean, timeless look that adds resale value to the place."

Tony had made the mistake of taking a deep sip of the cold beer, and found himself choking with laughter at Matteo's recitation.

Slay didn't have that problem. "Brother, do you even hear yourself right now? You're a fucking Home Depot commercial!" he crowed.

Matteo shrugged and sipped his beer, supremely unconcerned.

"The real problem here is that Matt's opened a can of worms," Dom said, twisting his head to look at his twin with a smirk. "And Heidi's caught the renovation bug now, too. Oh, speaking of which, none of you happen to know anything about Brazilian cherry versus bamboo flooring for the kitchen, do you? Bamboo's cheaper, but I'm wondering about durability."

"Shit, Dom. You, too? You and Matt should get your own show. The Renovation Twins." Slay ran a hand over the stubble on his shaved head and chuckled at his own joke.

"Identical twins who renovate houses? Been done," Tony informed him. And when Slay turned to look at him skeptically, Tony shrugged. "No, seriously. I've seen it. Tess loves those shows."

"You and Tess, huh?" Slay asked, giving Tony a significant look, a look that asked if Tony knew what Tess was all about and if he was prepared to meet her needs.

"Yeah," Tony said firmly. "Me and Tess."

God, he loved the way that sounded.

Slay nodded once in acceptance... then shook his head ruefully at the implications.

"Christ. I'm the last man standing. All alone on this little island called Sanity," Slay said to the ceiling. "So you're gonna be plunking down a wad of cash next, Ton? Redoing your living room? Turning your spare room into a sex playroom?"

A sex playroom? Hmm... now that was an idea with potential. A room dedicated to spanking Tess's luscious ass? Every home should have one.

The regret was clear in his voice as he said, "'Fraid not, man. I rent."

Slay burst out laughing.

"Three guys, led around by the balls by their females," he taunted. "Honest to God, you will never catch me bending over backwards to please a woman, no matter how pretty she is."

Tony looked at Dom, and then at Matteo. All three exchanged knowing smirks as they sipped their beer.

Slay could say whatever the hell he wanted, but he was totally missing the point. Dom and Matteo weren't bending over backwards to please anyone—Tony had been there and done that with Val, so he could say that with certainty. They were taking care of their women. And helping their women build them a home. There was nothing more important than that.

Tony was about to open his mouth to say so, when the phone in his back pocket started to chime with an incoming text message. He shifted forward to retrieve it.

"Ah, speaking of the little lady," Slay said, crossing one ankle over the other and stacking his hands behind his head. "She keeping tabs on you, honey bunch?"

"Jealous, Slater? 'Cause I'm noticing your phone's conspicuously *silent*," Tony remarked with mock sympathy. "You need pointers, man? I could totally help you with your game."

Slay flipped him off.

The guys started chuckling, ribbing Slay for his track record with women, but Tony was only listening with half an ear. Because when he checked the screen, he saw the message wasn't from Tess. It was from Val. *Again.*

Tony, I just need five minutes of your time. That's all. Tell me when and where.

Shit.

As he read the words, his mind projected them in the wheedling, petulant voice he associated with Val. His shoulders tensed and his gut churned instinctively.

For the thousandth time, he contemplated just blocking her fucking number... but it seemed so cowardly, as though she still had power over him, as though he still cared what she had to say. Nothing could be further from the truth.

He'd been an ignorant idiot when it came to Val. He'd been afraid to speak up, afraid that the only alternative to caving to her every whim was to be a misogynistic bastard. He'd thought that giving in was the only way to prove he was a decent guy, to show he cared. Over the past few months, Tess had taught him differently. Now he knew that being strong, dominant, and firmly in control wasn't remotely the same as being abusive—it was nurturing and protective, when you had the right partner. And now he was happier and more confident than he had been in fucking years.

Still... there was not one single part of him that wanted to have a conversation with Val or lay eyes on her again, either.

He'd been an idiot. And every communication from Val was a reminder of that.

"Tony?" Dom said, concern in his voice.

Tony glanced up. "Yeah?"

"What's up?" Dom asked, nodding at the phone in Tony's hand.

"Ah... nothing," Tony said with a shrug, putting the phone face down on the arm of the chair. "No big deal."

"Look on your face says different," Matteo disagreed. "Things okay with Tess?"

Tony grimaced, then sighed. "It's not Tess. It's Val."

"Val?" Dom sounded appalled. "Jesus, why?"

Tony shook his head. "Dunno. She's messaged me a couple of times over the past few weeks."

Or maybe it had been longer. A month? More?

Matt scowled. "Bitch needs to clue in to the fact that you're done."

Tony nodded. She really did.

"What does she want?" Slay asked.

"No clue." Tony shrugged. "I'm not returning her messages."

He saw Matt, Dom, and Slay exchange glances.

"What?" he demanded. "I don't want to talk to her. Besides which, I'm with Tess now. I'm not going around talking to Val behind her back. I don't even want her to know that Val has been texting me."

Which was the other reason why Val's texts set him on edge. He remembered all too clearly the way Tess had reacted when she'd caught sight of Val's message in his office a few weeks ago. The hurt on her face, the betrayal. And that was before they'd even been together! So, *no way* was he gonna mess shit up with Tess by clearing the air with Val.

A tense moment passed, in which each man stared fixedly at his beer or his shoes.

"Rethink that strategy, Ton," Dom said finally. "Not the part about being with Tess, but the part about not telling her. And the part about ignoring Val. One thing I'll give that woman, she's fucking tenacious. Like a dog with a bone."

"Like a *pit bull*, Matteo corrected, draining the last of his beer. "She won't drop it. You know this."

"So I give in, give her what she wants?" Tony demanded. Hell no. He would *not* roll over for that woman ever again.

"You ask her what she wants, then you tell her you're blocking her forever," Dom said. "Your terms."

Tony blew out a breath. Clearly, his current approach—ignoring her and hoping she'd go away—wasn't working, so maybe he did need a new strategy. "I'll think about it," he allowed.

Dom nodded. He started to say something else, but then a commotion in the entryway had all four of them turning their heads.

"Be careful of the painting on the wall, John!" Hillary exclaimed anxiously.

"Jesus," John grumbled, coming into view carrying an extremely tall, curved metal floor lamp. Hillary was trailing behind him, blonde curls bouncing and hands outstretched, as though waiting to catch the lamp if it fell.

"Come help me pick a lamp, John! You have the best taste, John! Can't do it without you, John!" John sing-songed. "Might've told me I was gonna be your pack mule, Hillary."

"Aw," Tess said, coming into view behind them, weighed down by several large bags labeled Bath and Home Emporium. Wisps of auburn hair fell from her ponytail to curl around her beautiful face, and her green sweater and jeans hugged her body in a way that made Tony squirm. "But if you hadn't come, we wouldn't have had this chance to admire your manly muscles! Hey, guys!" she said to the room at large.

John set the lamp down on the floor near the chair where Matteo sat.

"That's true," he said with a resigned sniff. Then turning a friendly smile on the assembled men, he said, "Afternoon, gents."

Dom, Tony, and Slay, replied with grunts, chin lifts, and beer-bottle salutes.

But Matteo didn't return the greeting. His eyes were on Hillary, who had crossed to the kitchen and was beginning to unpack the bags Tessa had hefted onto the counter.

"Tink," he growled.

Hillary looked up immediately, chagrined.

"You're upset about how much stuff I got, aren't you? Matt, I know it looks like a lot," she placated. "I swear, I stayed in budget." She moved her index finger in a cross over her heart.

Matteo shook his head slowly. "That's great, baby, but I'm not worried about the budget."

Hillary blinked. "Oh. Well, I only got the things we discussed. Towels and, um… cookie sheets, and uh…" Hillary's voice trailed off as Matteo shook his head once again.

"Whatever you want, babe. Don't care about that either," he said.

"Well then why are you looking at me like that?" she asked nervously.

Matteo pursed his lips. "Let's see," he pondered thoughtfully, eyes to the ceiling. "Could it be that you just walked in the door, and then right past me, and didn't say hello at all?"

"Didn't say… Oh!" Hillary said in surprise. Then she bit her lip as though she was fighting a smile. "I did do that, didn't I?"

Someone, Tony couldn't tell if it was Dom or Slay, snickered. Tessa leaned back against the counter and smiled. Tony caught Tess's eye and gave her a wink, and her smile widened.

"You did," Matteo confirmed with a smirk.

Hillary nodded seriously. She shuffled toward his chair, then leaned over at the waist and pressed a dutiful kiss to his lips. "Hello, Matteo."

"Sassy," Matteo grumbled when Hillary straightened, but his eyes were dancing. He caught her wrist and tugged her down to sit on the arm of his chair. "We'll discuss this later."

Hillie's saucy smile that said she was looking forward to it.

Tony lifted his hand and gestured for Tess to come to him. She rolled her eyes, but eagerly came forward and mirrored Hillary's actions, bending toward him and pressing a kiss to his lips.

"Hello, Tony," she parroted.

Tony snorted... and reached around to deliver a sound smack to her ass. "Keep it up, Tessa, and we can discuss *your* sassy attitude right here and *now*," he muttered.

"Tony!" she squeaked, blushing as she glanced from Slay to Dom to Matteo, but she didn't offer the slightest protest when Tony tugged her down to sit on his lap.

Dom and Matt pretended not to have heard Tony's comment, but Slay looked at them intently for a moment, as though thinking about something, before nodding and glancing away.

"Where's the rest of the shopping expedition?" Dom asked Hillary. "Was there not enough room for Heidi and Paul in the car with all your bags?"

Hillary looked at Matteo, and then glanced quickly at the other faces in the living room, before chuckling nervously. "Uh...Well..."

Matteo's eyes widened. "Are you kidding me?"

"No! I mean... of course they *fit* in the *car*, honey! Paul was driving us in his truck for goodness sake!" Hillary protested. "It's just that, um... they also had those side tables we agreed on for the bedroom, Matt, and they were on clearance! Half price!"

Matteo pursed his lips. "I know you love a bargain, babe. But aren't those the same tables we already discussed? The ones that we agreed that I would go with you to purchase next week, so that I could carry them?"

Hillary looked down at her hands. "Yeah, those," she agreed, then tried to explain. "But there was only one set left! And they totally would've been gone by next week."

"My cell's been on all day," Matteo noted.

Hillary squeezed her eyes shut. "Didn't think of that."

"Uh huh. Sounds like we will have *several* things to discuss later," Matteo said, only half joking.

Hillary nodded and winced, suddenly subdued.

Tess buried her face in Tony's neck, and he would swear she was hiding a smile.

"Where are the tables now, honey?" Matt asked, his tone gentler now.

"In Paul's truck downstairs. Heidi is waiting with him," Hillie told him.

"I'll go help Paul," Matt said, ruffling Hillary's curls with one big hand.

"Nah, you wait here," Dom said, standing up quickly. "Slay and I have got this. Besides, it's time I got Heidi home. Away from all you dangerous influences." He gave John a knowing look and shot Tessa a wink.

He paused to give Hillary a kiss on top of her head and clap Matt on the shoulder as he and Slay made their way to the door.

"Oh! Before I forget!" Hillary said, twisting in her chair to look at the departing men. "Alice called me today. Alice Cavanaugh, the bartender at The Club, who's also working for Tony," she explained, for Dom's benefit.

Dom nodded in recognition.

"There's a fundraiser at her kid's school tomorrow. Some kind of pumpkin festival thing, with all kinds of baked goods and sack races and a Ferris wheel. Apparently she's supposed to sell a certain number of tickets to stay in the PTO's good graces," Hillary scoffed.

"Because the woman doesn't have enough to do, raising an awesome kid by herself and working two jobs to support him," Tess said. "PTO idiots and their skewed priorities."

Alice had brought her six-year-old son, Charlie, to the restaurant on a couple of occasions over the past few weeks, and everyone had fallen for him. If his big blue eyes and blond curls didn't melt you, his serious, earnest little personality would. Tony knew Tess had fallen harder for the boy than anyone, and witnessing the way Alice killed herself every day to make sure Charlie had the best of everything had cemented Tess's good opinion of the woman. Devoted mothers were not something his Tess took for granted.

Tony could feel the tension in her body now, and knew the situation was hitting a little close to home.

"I know, hon," Hillary agreed softly. "And that's why I thought maybe we could go to support her. Paul and John and all of us girls are down, but we couldn't commit without asking you guys. What do you think?" Hillary turned imploring eyes on Dom, Slay, and Matt in turn.

Matt shrugged with wide eyes, as though participating in a kids' festival was a given. "Of course. Dom and I haven't had a chance to test out our mad three-legged-race skills for years. I'm getting rusty."

Dom rolled his eyes. "I'll pass my spot to Hillary, bro. But Heidi and I are in. You had me at baked goods."

"Yeah, I know someone who can't resist a pumpkin muffin," Tony said, tickling Tess lightly and making her jump. "We're in."

"Oh, awesome!" Hillary said, clasping her hands. "Alice will be psyched. What about you, Slay?"

All eyes in the room turned to Slay, who looked at Hillary like a deer caught in headlights. He rubbed his hands back and forth over his head and cleared his throat nervously. "Well, I dunno…"

"It sounds like fun," Hillary wheedled. "And it would mean a lot to Alice and Charlie."

"Yeah?" Slay nodded. "Okay, then. I'll be there." And then he all but ran out the door.

The six-foot-five giant of a bouncer who stared down drunk assholes at The Club on a regular basis was scared of a school fair? Slay was a good guy, but Tony couldn't help but think he was a little whacked, too.

"Tess and John, before you leave can you help me put this stuff away?" Hillary pleaded, motioning towards the bags on the counter.

Tess moved to get off Tony's lap, but he held her in place for just a moment… just long enough to brush a kiss over her lips. Cherry lip-gloss and Tess.

Christ. When had cherries become an aphrodisiac?

"You have ten minutes, then we're leaving," he warned.

She nodded quickly and scurried to the kitchen.

"Hey, Tony, you got a minute?" Matt whispered once she was out of immediate ear shot. He stood and motioned Tony towards the hallway that led to the bedrooms.

"What's up?" Tony asked, curious and amused at the sudden cloak-and-dagger.

"Man, I need your help," Matt whispered, once they were out of earshot. "I'm trying to plan a surprise party for Tink, and I don't want anyone to know about it."

"A party? What kind of party?"

"A celebrating party. She just sold a book," Matteo told him. And though the words were simple, Matt's beaming smile and the delight in his voice told the tale. He was beyond proud of his woman.

"Ah, man! That's awesome," Tony said, grinning. "I should congratulate her."

But Matt grabbed his arm when he tried to leave. "Nah, she doesn't want anyone to know until the contract is signed. That's why I want to plan something secret. At *Cara*."

Tony nodded. "We can do that!"

"Awesome. I knew you'd come through for me. But I'm serious, man. I know you'll want to confess it all to Tess and clear your conscience, but you can't! For her sake! It'd kill her!" Matteo lowered his voice even further, and whispered. "She'd be dying to tell Hillary, and I know Tink would catch on."

Tony rolled his eyes. "Fine," he said. "I won't. But I hate keeping secrets."

Matt snorted. "Unless it's about Val."

Tony scowled. Asshole.

"Seriously, man, you need to call Val. Tell her this is it, and things are over, for good. No more text messages… no more communications, period. You can't let her string you along this way. If Tess finds out…"

"Tess *won't* find out, okay? I'll take care of everything," Tony assured him.

And he would. Somehow. Everything would be fine.

When Hillie had said that Alice needed to raise funds for her kid's school, Tony had somehow pictured some tiny little fair at a regular suburban elementary school, like the one Tony himself had attended. He had *not* expected a setup that rivaled a theme park in terms of size and scope. But then again, he hadn't expected that her kid attended Pevrell and Brahms, once of the most exclusive private schools in town.

He couldn't deny, it made for a pretty scene. The school was a trio of red brick buildings covered in ivy that was slowly turning color, flanked by rolling fields of lush green grass where picturesque white booths and display tables were set up. Further back, the whirling and clanging of the rides and games mixed with the sounds of childish giggles. The air was chilly in that clear, crisp late-October-in-New-England way, where the sun was still high and warm, but the cold breeze reminded you that the weather isn't gonna hold, and you'll be in for a storm before long.

This was the foreboding thought in Tony's mind as he made his way across the packed parking lot to the "fairgrounds."

"We are never going to find Heidi and Dom and everyone in this crowd," he told the silent woman at his side.

She murmured noncommittally, which was typical of the responses she'd given him for the past twenty-four hours. He sighed and scrubbed a hand over his head in frustration.

"I'm gonna ask you one more time, Tessa. What the fuck is wrong?" he demanded.

In truth, he already knew. Things had been fine between them—more than fine!—until yesterday afternoon when he'd fucked up by giving her that very public swat and reprimand, right in Matteo's living room. Tess was a private person—how many times had she insisted on staying professional and keeping their distance in front of other people? Without thinking, he'd crossed that line.

And if that was the problem, he was prepared to discuss it with her, to find out what the underlying issue was, to figure out how they should proceed…

But first the woman had to fucking talk to him.

He'd tried everything he could think of to get her to open up, from joking to threatening spankings. She'd answered him the same way every time. "I don't want to talk right now, and I don't want a spanking. Please leave me alone."

He hadn't the first fucking clue how to proceed from there.

Up until now, every spanking he'd administered had been with her enthusiastic agreement. Hell, she'd been begging for it. But now, when he felt like she most needed it, like *they* most needed it, to get them back on track and centered, it seemed like she'd withdrawn her consent. And he couldn't do anything without her okay, could he?

So they'd moved through the night and day, with her not talking or touching him or even meeting his eyes. And, by now, he was annoyed.

Oh, what the hell. He was fucking *pissed*.

They approached the entrance gate, and Tony handed over their ticket money to an incredibly thin, fake-looking blonde wearing tight leggings and those weird furry boot things.

"And whose list should I put you on?" she asked giving him a bright smile.

"Pardon?" Tess asked, her eyes narrowed.

"Which child are you here for?" the woman elaborated, her smile slipping several notches as she evaluated Tess's outfit—a fitted flannel shirt and another pair of those ass-hugging jeans that made Tony want to drop to his knees and thank God he was a man... even when he was ready to spank the hell out of her.

Clearly the woman was jealous of what she saw, because her lips took on a pinched look and she exchanged a sidelong glance with the other woman at the table, a fake-looking brunette in a pumpkin sweater.

"We're here for Charlie Cavanaugh," Tess challenged, as though daring the woman to say a word against the boy.

"I see," the blonde said, making a note on a sheet of paper. "Well, I'm sure Miss Cavanaugh will appreciate that. She's a bit behind!" She exchanged another glance with pumpkin-woman, and they both gave a weird half-chuckle that put Tony's back up.

But for Tess, that chuckle acted like a spark to tinder.

"Behind in what?" Tess demanded.

The pumpkin lady didn't even pretend to be friendly. "Behind in her fundraising requirement. All of the children on scholarships are required to raise a certain amount through fundraisers. Somehow, Miss Cavanaugh has managed to skate by until now, but this year those of us on the fundraising committee are being forced to take a hard line." She narrowed her eyes. "For the good of the school."

"Is that right?" Tess whispered. "Well, then..."

Tess grabbed her wallet from her back pocket and counted out $200, slapping it down on the table in front of the woman. "Let me contribute *that* in Charlie's name. For the good of the school," she said.

Pumpkin lady gaped. Blondie looked like she'd been sucking on something sour.

Tony had never felt such an overpowering urge to kiss someone—it was almost scary. Because, God, if she was that fiercely protective of a boy she hardly knew, how would she be with their own kids?

His mind stuttered to a halt.

Their own kids.

Little Tessas with hazel eyes and sassy smiles. Little Tonys with Tess's reddish hair.

Holy shit.

He wanted that. For the first time in his life, he wanted that.

But only with Tessa.

"Hey, Tess. Tony." Slay said in greeting as he came up to the ticket counter. "Christ, this thing's bigger than I expected."

Tony was still speechless, but Tess had no problem explaining.

"This... *lady*... here says that Charlie needs to raise more money. He's a *scholarship kid* who's behind in his *fundraising goal*. For the good of the school." The look she gave Slay clearly showed her disgust at this idea.

Slay's sharp brown eyes seemed to comprehend the scene all at once, and his disgust rivaled hers.

"Huh. That right?" Slay grabbed his wallet and removed a wad of cash, handing it to pumpkin lady with a hard expression.

"Oh, but this is way too much..." the woman sputtered in protest.

"Then apply it to his fundraising goal for next year," Slay said. And without another word, he strolled through the gate and into the fair.

Tony and Tess followed.

"Holy shit, did you see that?" Tess crowed, her annoyance with him forgotten in light of what they'd just seen. "Oh, I am serving that man free drinks and meals for the rest of his natural life! He must've given her five hundred dollars!"

"Yeah, that's... awesome..." Tony agreed, still shell-shocked by his own thoughts.

"You have no idea what it's like, Tony, to be the kid who

always has to wear the castoff clothes, whose mom can't raise money for the class field trip or to pay the fees for the advanced classes and exams! Oh, it felt so fucking good to be able to do that for him!" Her cheeks were pink, her eyes sparkling with emotion.

Christ, she was ferocious and gorgeous. He'd known he loved her, but now he knew he couldn't live without her. He needed to tell her and make things right between them. And he needed to not fuck it up.

He cupped her cheek in one hand.

"Tess," he began hesitantly. "I need to talk to you. I…"

"Tony! Buddy, good to see you," Paul said, coming up behind him and clapping him on the shoulder. "I've been looking for you everywhere! Can I talk to you for a second?"

Tess looked away and Tony exhaled sharply, trying to hold onto his patience.

"Paul, man, can you give us a minute?" Tony asked.

"Tess, Alice is working the balloon booth over there," Paul said, by way of answer. "Charlie's with her, and he's dying to go on some of the big kid rides. Maybe you could take him!"

"Uh… okay?" Tess said, looking from Paul to Tony in confusion.

Tony shrugged. He had no idea what Paul's issue was.

"Great! Just head over, and I'll return this guy to you in a couple of minutes, honey!" Paul told her.

As soon as she left, Tony turned to Paul. "What the *fuck*, man?" Tony asked.

"You can kill me later, Tony," Paul said, dropping his smile. "But you are not gonna fucking believe who is here right now."

"Who? And why did you have to get rid of Tess?"

"You'll see," Paul said grimly.

A moment later, Paul led him to a booth where a group of younger children were lining up to throw hoops over bottles to win prizes. And just beyond them, perched on the edge of a craft table… was Val.

Shit.

Her hair was the same bright blonde it had always been, and just as fashionably styled. Her makeup was flawless, as always, and her outfit no doubt cost more than his monthly rent. And she smiled in an artful, practiced way that set his teeth on edge.

"What are you doing here?" he demanded.

Val stood as he approached and sucked in a breath. She licked her lips nervously.

"I… I had no idea you would be here," she stammered. "I'm not stalking you or anything. I'm… here with my… with a friend." She gestured to one side, and Tony noticed a stocky man sporting tattoos, motorcycle boots, and a watchful expression. "I just saw Paul and Heidi, and I thought maybe you'd be here, so I asked."

She looked at the man again, and he nodded in an encouraging way. She continued, "I wanted to say…"

"I think we've said everything we need to say to one another, Val," Tony told her flatly, crossing his arms over his chest.

She nodded seriously. "I get it. I do. I just wanted to apologize. I said a lot of things to you that weren't true. I let my insecurities drive me to do a lot of things I'm not proud of. I was hateful to you… and to Tess," she whispered, her eyes flicking to the watchful man once again.

Tony sucked in a breath. In all the months they'd been together, he couldn't remember Val uttering more than a cursory apology for anything.

"And I…" She took a deep breath and reached into her purse. "I've been carrying around this check for weeks. A month, maybe?" She gave a little laugh. "I've been waiting, just in case I had a chance to give it to you."

"A check?" He blinked. Jesus, had he been sucked into an alternate dimension at some point?

"Yeah, I... I have a really good job now," she said proudly. "In marketing. It's challenging, but fun. And it pays well." She took another deep breath and smiled—a real smile, this time, that lit up her eyes in a way Tony hadn't known was possible. "Anyway, I know I was really bad about money when we were together. I bought a lot of stupid stuff." She pursed her lips and shook her head. "But Mike and I are moving in together." She gave the tattooed man her real smile, and Tony saw the man's lip twitch. "So I sold all my shit."

"You sold..."

"Almost all of it, yeah," she confirmed. "All the designer dresses and shoes and purses, all the jewelry, my little Fiat. It was really crappy in the snow anyway. And it just seemed right that you get half the cut since you bought half the stuff."

Tony felt his jaw hanging open. He looked from Val to Mike the Mystery Man in concern. Had Val lost her mind? Was she okay? Was the guy forcing her to do this? Not Tony's problem, and didn't *want* to care, damn it, but he still did, to a certain extent.

"No, I haven't decided to swear off all worldly goods and join a cult," Val told him with a laugh, as though she could read his mind. "But I've definitely made a lot of changes. Seems like you have too," she said with a smile. "I know what I *need* now. And what I can't live without. And I'm happy. I figured out that when you're happy, you don't need a lot of stuff." Mike raised one eyebrow and gave Val a measured look. Val bit her lip to cover her smile. "Or, you don't need *as much* stuff, at least," she amended.

Then she looked at Tony and threw up her hands. "So that's it!" she said. "That's all I wanted to say. I wish you well, I'm sorry I was an insecure, jealous shrew, and please take this check!"

She giggled at the expression on Tony's face. "Mike told me I needed to apologize in person, otherwise I would've just mailed it. But I've gotta say, it's worth it just to see your expression."

Tony stared at the check. Holy shit.

He looked from the check, to Val, to Mike the Mystery Dude. "I seriously don't know what to say, Val."

"Nothing to say, Tony," she told him gently. "I was too insecure to know what I needed, and you were too hesitant to give it to me. But it's okay, because now we can move on. In a good way. In a healthy way."

Tony nodded. "I hope… I'm glad… I want you to be happy," he told her.

"Same goes, Tony. Will you tell Tess what I said?"

Tony nodded slowly. Maybe. Eventually. After he'd processed this surreal experience.

Val smiled. Then she stepped forward and planted a kiss on his cheek. Tony's hands instinctively reached out and gripped her by the shoulders.

"Take care of yourself," he told her.

Then he and Mike exchanged nods… and Val was gone from his life. Forever.

And damn, but he felt freer somehow.

"What the fuck was that?" Paul marveled.

"*Who* the fuck was that?" Tony joked. "It *looked* a lot like Val, but I'm not convinced. What do you know about alien abduction?"

"I'm not positive, but I think I've seen that guy before," Paul said, and Tony caught a thread of amusement in his voice. "No wonder Val finally got her shit straightened out."

Tony's eyes widened as he stared at Paul. "Tell me you don't know him from The Club."

Paul snickered. "No, but we do have friends in common. I think his name's Mike Federico. He's not a classic dom, keeps to himself. Haven't seen him around for a while. But, yeah."

Tony shook his head. None of his business. He couldn't process that information, and he didn't want to.

He needed to get back to Tess and tell her everything that

had happened, everything that he felt. He needed to kiss her. He needed to make things right between them again.

But he had one stop to make first.

"Let's head back to the ticket counter," he told Paul, glancing down at the check in his hands. "See if we can't pay Charlie Cavanaugh's fundraising requirement for the rest of his fucking life." On behalf of Tess and Nora and all the other kids who couldn't.

Chapter 9

Tess almost caved. After she saw Tony with Slay and Paul, and way those guys handed over money to fund Charlie's fundraiser, it made her cry. She had to excuse herself and ran to the ladies' room inside the school, wiping her tears and doing the deep breathing and quick pacing she'd learned so that she wouldn't lose her shit in public. Smoothing her shaking hands over her jeans, she felt the bumps of scars on her thighs. Her fingers curled into fists, the nails digging into her flesh so hard it made her wince.

The temptation to hurt herself had never been stronger.

She'd never avoided the temptation so long.

Between the stress about Nora, and the worries she had with Tony, and now going to bat for Charlie, which dredged up the memory of every single school fundraiser she'd struggled through as a child, she was a freaking basket case. What she really needed was a good spanking, and not a handful of swats on her ass when she was bent over in bed seconds before he took her, but an honest-to-god session that left her helpless, sore, and flying as high as a kite.

But the only guy she would ever submit to like that was out

there doing *who knew what* with his *supposedly*-ex-girlfriend. Could she even trust him?

First, text messages on his phone left *right there*, plain as day, for anyone to see when he threw his phone beside the bed. Val was messaging him again? And okay, so maybe Val was just a nutcase who didn't know to leave well enough alone. He couldn't *tell* her? But then she'd overheard the tail end of his conversation at Matteo's house yesterday. *Don't tell Tess. You only keep secrets about Val. Tess won't find out.* And it confirmed her suspicions. He *had* been in touch with Val. But then to have the nerve to meet *up* with Val? And *kiss* her? Tessa braced herself on the vanity in the bathroom and stared at her reflection.

You haven't gotten this far by being a pushover, or a bitch, Tessa Damon, she told herself. *You've been honest, and worked your ass off, and built solid friendships. And that isn't going to change now.*

Submissive though she was, she did not put up with shit. Just because she liked to submit didn't mean she could be walked over, or taken for granted.

She and Tony needed to have a talk.

When she joined him and Paul at the cotton candy stand, Tony twirled off a piece of candy onto his finger and tried to feed it to her. Closing her lips tightly, she turned away.

"Ohh no, thanks," she said. "Way too sticky and sweet. You ready to go soon?"

Tony's jaw clenched as he shoved the rest of the candy into his mouth. He raised an eyebrow at her.

Paul looked from one to the other, his eyes flicking over them as if probing, but then he shook his head. "Gotta go," he said. "Oh, Tony, we'll talk more about the plans, right?"

Tony frowned at Paul. "Yeah, later," he said. "Not now."

What the *hell?* What *plans?*

Paul nodded and left. Tony inhaled, turning to Tess, but she was already *done*. Already *fed up*.

"More secrets, Tony? Huh? More stuff to hide from me?"

He frowned, his eyes darkening. "Huh? What the hell are you talking about?"

She exhaled angrily. "Forget it! Let's get the hell out of here."

Tony threw the rest of the cotton candy in a nearby trashcan before he stalked over to her. She felt real fear for a quick second. She couldn't recall ever seeing him so angry, unless it was the time at the restaurant when a stalker had preyed on Hillary right under his nose. As he marched toward her, she backpedaled, until she was flat up against the backside of a little trailer that sold French fries. He towered over her and his eyes were furious.

"What is going *on*? I've *had* it, Tessa. Had it! I've tried everything I know. I've tried talking and cajoling and insisting, and you won't out with it. What the *fuck*?" he hissed. His cheeks were red with anger as both hands went to her shoulders, pinning her firmly against the wall. All she wanted to do was shove him away.

"Not here," she hissed back. "Let's go."

With one quick tug of her hair, he had her head pulled back and he was whispering in her ear.

"I've never wanted to spank anyone so bad in my life," he growled. Then he released her as he stalked to the parking lot. She gasped, still angry at him, but now furious that he had the nerve to turn her on in the middle of all this.

"You don't do that to me!" she whispered angrily. "You do *not do that to me!*"

He merely turned to face her, lips pursed and brows raised as he continued to stalk to the car.

"We'll see what I can and cannot do when we get back to our place."

But this time, it was fury that she felt coursing through her. She wanted to smack him, or shake him, and her hands shook with the pent-up anger.

"We. Will. *Not!*" she said, stomping her foot. "It will be on… my terms! I'm getting *my way*!"

It frustrated her how her vocabulary evaporated when she was furious. Even she knew she sounded like a spoiled child.

They stood beside his car now. He glared at her silently and beeped the key that unlocked the doors. He pointed wordlessly for her to get in. She stomped her foot and crossed her arms, finally opening the door and slamming it shut behind her. In another time and place, she'd have found their childish exchange comical, but she was too pissed to see the humor.

Tony had insisted on driving and Tessa was grateful, because she needed some time to think things over. She wanted a good, solid, strategic approach for how she was going to handle this discussion. Tess knew it would better to just get to the heart of the issue with a direct question.

"Why did you kiss Val?"

"Why didn't you tell me she was texting you?"

But she wanted a few minutes to compose herself before she talked to him.

"I've got to go to *Cara* first," he muttered. "Left some stuff."

"What did you leave?"

"Stuff."

She snorted. "Of course you did."

"You're being a total brat."

"You're being a total jerk."

"Am not!"

"Are too!"

"Whatever!"

They fumed silently all the way to *Cara*. He careened into the parking lot and came to an abrupt stop in his usual parking space.

"You stay right there," he ordered, slamming the door and hitting the locks on his keys.

"Yes, *sir!*" she growled.

Even in the moment, she was sorta thankful Tony wasn't like the other doms she knew. Someone like Matteo or Dom might take her across their knees without giving her a chance to talk, and the thought of getting spanked by Tony when she was so mad at him made her feel even worse. *He* was the one who was wrong, not her.

"Maybe I should become a switch," she muttered under her breath. "Maybe *he's* the one who needs to be spanked." She snorted to herself, then, as the door to the car yanked open.

"Tess. You need to come with me."

She turned to look at him, her lips still pursed and angry, but he looked different now, not as pissed off. Confused, she shook her head.

"What? Why?"

He blew out a breath and ran a hand through his hair. "Just come with me."

Her anger flared again. "You know what? No. You don't get to just order me around like that," she began.

"It's your mother."

She froze, one livid index finger pointed angrily at him suspended in mid-air. She dropped her hands onto her lap.

"What?" she whispered.

"She's inside with Nora, and she wants to talk to you. Let's go."

Tessa closed her eyes and shook her head.

"Put down whatever shit's eating you up right now and we'll talk about it later."

Fine.

She opened the car door and slammed it shut behind her, refusing his hand and to even walk beside him, stalking ahead of him.

"Tess," he began, but she marched past him.

She'd gotten this far without Tony.

She didn't need him now.

Tessa inhaled as she entered *Cara*. The familiar smell of tomatoes, garlic, and basil eased her nerves a bit, as the employees working murmured their greeting. She nodded to all of them, stepping past the kitchen to the main dining area, and she froze.

There was her mother, sitting at a table. She looked as if she'd taken some time to doll herself up for the evening. Her hair was brushed, at least, even if she was squeezed into a too-tight top and her makeup did nothing to cover up her shifty eyes and pursed lips. Tessa felt her stomach squeeze. Nora was sitting awkwardly on the other side of the table.

"Hey, kiddo," Tessa said to Nora, forcing herself to stay cool, calm, and collected as she slid into a chair between the two, mostly to avoid causing a scene.

Nora's face was pinched, caught somewhere between being a confident woman and scared little girl. Her eyes flickered over Tessa and then back to her mom. "Mom came to visit," she said, as if Tessa somehow needed to be told. "She insisted on staying to see you," she added apologetically.

Tess looked to her mother. "Is that right?"

Her mother barely nodded in return as Tess leaned closer and lowered her voice. "Why are you here?"

Her mom's eyes darted from Nora to Tess, and back again. "Well, first off, I came to take my daughter home with me."

Tess blinked, then her eyes narrowed. "Not happening."

"Yes it is," her mother insisted. "Nora is a minor and I am her mother."

"This is not the time or the place for this discussion," Tess said, her eyes taking in the packed dining room. She felt Tony come to stand behind her chair, one hand resting on her shoulder, and despite everything that had imploded between them, it was his presence that allowed her to speak calmly through the anger and fear that gripped her. She was pretty sure the correct time to discuss Nora moving back to their mother's shitty apartment was *never*.

"Oh, there won't *be* a discussion," Desiree said smugly. "Nora will do what I tell her. Oh, and while we're at it? Nora would also like to give her notice. She won't be working here any more. Her stepfather's found her another job."

Tess fumed. *Stepfather.* Yeah, because Roger was so fucking *paternal* when it came to Nora.

It was Tony who leaned around Tess and spoke into her mother's ear in a deceptively pleasant tone. "I think you'll want to reconsider based on what we've heard from Nora. How do you think the police would react if Nora told them what she's seen in your house?"

"You bitch!" Desiree told Nora, her eyes flashing. "You fucking opened your mouth?"

Nora flushed bright red. "They came to pick me up after you destroyed all of my things! And I've told you a million times that I don't like the way Roger looks at me!" Her voice was filled with hurt and not a small amount of guilt.

Tess laid a hand on Nora's arm. "You have every right to feel safe in your own home," she told the younger girl.

Nora looked at her briefly, and then back at their mother. "I don't want to go," she told Desiree.

Desiree shook her head. "And you'd do it, like they say? You'd rat me out to the fucking cops? Tell them about Roger and the boys? You'd do that to your own mother?"

Nora hesitated for a moment, then took a deep breath and nodded. "You want me to let them kiss me… and worse. How can *you* do that to your own *daughter*?"

Desiree looked shocked and scared. Then she turned furious eyes on Tess. "I guess you're pretty proud of yourself, huh? Not the first fucking clue how to be loyal to your family, or how to be a decent person, and now you're training your sister to follow in your footsteps." She turned to Tony. "Don't think I don't see what's going on here. My crazy daughter let you in her pants, huh? Be warned. *You* look like a nice guy and *she* is a fucking toxic, psycho *bitch*."

Desiree almost screamed the last part, and Tess felt shame flood her chest. The temptation to reach out and slap her mother's face was almost overwhelming.

"Out," Tony ordered. He grabbed Desiree by her elbow and lifted her to her feet. His face was frozen in a calm mask, but Tess could tell by his rapid breathing that only the fear of causing her more embarrassment prevented him from lifting the older woman in his capable hands and *throwing* her bodily from the restaurant. Instead, he continued to hold her elbow and forcefully walked her to the door.

To Tessa's shock, her mother actually walked with him, though the woman couldn't help sashaying as she walked and drawing the eye of every guest in the restaurant.

Damn her.

Tessa stayed at the table, reminding herself that making even more of a scene by running after her mother, tackling her to the ground, and slapping the crap out of her, would not actually help anyone, no matter how satisfying the fantasy was.

She grabbed Nora's hand as Tony smiled widely and leaned down to say something to her mother that made Desiree stomp out the front door. Tony turned to walk back to their table, still grinning for the benefit of those watching.

When he came to her, she and Nora both stood, and Tony put his arm around Nora's shoulders, guiding her back to the kitchen area. "Tess, you take Nora home," he said. "And I will be there as soon as I can. Maybe order something to eat," he suggested, giving Nora a gentle wink. "I won't even complain if it's not Italian."

They were at the employee room now, and Nora mechanically grabbed her things. "I'll spread the word to the rest of the staff that your mom isn't welcome at our establishment. No one comes here and threatens my employees and gets away with it."

Nora nodded and went to wave goodbye to the kitchen staff.

He walked them to the back lot where Tess had parked her car earlier before riding with Tony to the fair.

Nora impulsively threw her arms around Tony's neck. "Thanks for getting her to leave," she whispered.

Tony waved this away with one hand. "It was the threat of you talking that got her to leave, not me. You're a brave girl, Nora the Explorer."

Nora hugged him once more, then stepped back.

"To be honest, I'm not sure if I would've been able to do it. To call the cops on her. I know she's awful, and I know she's a bitch, but there were times when I was a kid that she wasn't so bad, you know?" Her eyes pleaded with Tess for understanding.

No, Tess didn't really know, and thought it more likely that this was something that Nora wanted to believe than something she actually remembered. Still, she nodded. "I get that it would be hard for you. Let's go home, kiddo."

Nora went around the far side of the car and slid into the passenger's seat.

When she was out of earshot, Tony said in a low voice, "I'm calling Matt. He and Slay have a lot of contacts in law enforcement, and I need to know what the deal is with this Roger asshole. I debated getting them involved when I first heard what happened to Nora, but now... You know, I meant what I said. No one comes into my place and threatens what's mine."

His *employees*, his *restaurant*. That's what he meant.

Tess sighed and looked up at Tony. Without Desiree and that immediate threat in front of them, she felt her anger and hurt rushing back in. She couldn't quite meet his eyes. "All right, I'll get Nora outta here. I can come back later to finish—"

"Nope," Tony said. "You won't. You'll head back with Nora and wait for me. You and I have some things to discuss tonight."

Things to discuss? Like how quickly she and Nora could be packed and out of his place?

If the situation at the fair hadn't been enough to show for

once and for all that she could never be good enough for Tony, the debacle in the dining room sure as hell had. *Her* mother, causing a scene in *his* restaurant. Now that he'd seen where she came from, there was no way he'd want anything to do with her. He wouldn't have any reason to keep pretending that his relationship with Val was over, or that Tess was more to him than the chick who kept his books and warmed his bed.

Tess wouldn't look at him, but merely shrugged. "Yeah," she agreed, pulling away from him. She felt sick to her stomach as she remembered everything. Val. Phone calls. Kisses.

Psycho bitch.

Why did Tony have to go and be all sweet now? And why did he have to swoop in and make everything better when she needed him?

"Tess," Tony began, but she was completely fried.

"Later," she mumbled, as she left.

Tess and Nora went back to Tony's place, and although Nora agreed when Tess called to order Chinese food, she had no interest in watching a movie or, God forbid, talking about what had happened. "I need to study for my bio test," she said. "And I don't want to fail my class because our mother's a psycho."

"I know, I know," Tess said. She was glad that Nora had agreed to stay home and study, even though she wished the girl would keep her company. For the first time in a very, very long time, she didn't want to be alone.

Alone. Always alone. Her hands shook.

The temptation to cut was overwhelming. She felt like an addict who needed a fix, something to control, something that would help her deal with the pain and loss of what she'd hoped for with all her heart.

But she dutifully left Nora in her room with her books, and

walked aimlessly into Tony's bedroom. Everything was tidy and perfect, just as she'd left it, even down to the pajama shorts and cami she'd stashed under her pillow. She hadn't known how badly things could change in one day, how everything that was right in the morning could turn so wrong by nightfall.

She and Tony were over. She'd have to find a place to live. Tess knew now that she'd have to leave *Cara*. If she and Tony were done, she'd have to find somewhere else to work. Where? How? She had no clue. She couldn't control any of it. She never fucking *could*.

She grabbed her pajamas from the bed and walked slowly into the bathroom. It felt like every move was an effort, her feet leaden and numb as she stripped. But as her clothes fell in the laundry basket, she caught sight of her reflection in the mirror that hung on the bathroom door. Gingerly, she ran her fingers along the edges of her scars, and her hands trembled harder.

She needed the release. She needed to feel the fear and know she could overcome it.

And she and Tony were done, so he would never know.

Flicking back the shower curtain so quickly the rungs clanged together, she turned the water on hot, so that the room filled with steam. Grabbing her razor from the shelf on the wall, she hiked up a leg. She took the razor and gently, ever so gently, drew the blade along her dry skin. She felt the scrape of it, watching her skin grow smooth and slightly pink. Running one finger along her skin, Tess inhaled. She looked at the blade, gleaming in the light of the bathroom, and ran it over her skin again. The trembling in her hands intensified. When she was younger, and would cut herself regularly, she had an arsenal of tools ready that she would sneak into the bathroom, or her bedroom, with the door shut. But now, she'd have to fiddle around with this blade, a fancy five-blade deal that was meant to prevent injury, not aid it.

Lips pursed together, Tessa drew the blade along her skin again, then tipped it, just enough so that the very edge glided along her upper thigh. Her head felt heady with anticipation, her palms grew sweaty and damp, and her breathing was ragged. The thump of her heart in the small bathroom seemed to be marching toward what she needed to do. She needed to feel the sharp sting and then release, needed to control this, take her mind off her fucked-up childhood and uselessness, her complete inability to maintain a healthy relationship with a guy, and the fears she had about what she would do now that she had *nothing* to fall back on. A sob caught in her throat as she replayed the scene with him and Val, and her hand twitched. She felt a gasp as the first drop of crimson blood dotted her thigh.

She was so caught up in her thoughts and fears and emotions, she never heard the door open.

"What the *hell* are you doing?" Tony bellowed from the doorway, making her drop the razor. It skidded into the tub, spinning, and she dropped her hands to cover her legs, but it was futile. He'd seen everything.

She didn't know a husky guy like him could move so fast. She was up and in his arms in seconds, as he marched her to the bedroom wordlessly. He tossed her on the bed, as she tried her best to make it seem she was doing something else.

"It's not what it looks like," she protested. He'd promised her under no uncertain terms that he would spank her good and hard, a real spanking, if she ever harmed herself, and he'd caught her right in the act. "Please, Tony. I'm not..." but she couldn't say it.

His eyes were furious, his lips thinned, red splotches on his cheek and his voice shook with anger.

"You're not *what?*" he said, his voice raising. "Then what *are* you doing, Tessa? You're not hurting yourself?"

"I'm not... I'm not *crazy*. I'm not *fucked up*. I'm not a fucking psycho like she says I am!" Tessa covered her face with her hands, as tears began to fall.

She heard him cross the room and sit on the bed. Lifting

Tessa up, he pulled her into his arms as she quietly wept. Gently, he tipped her head back and kissed her forehead before he pulled her head down to his chest.

"God, Tess," he said, and it seemed he was trying to quell his anger. "You're not psycho, honey. You're hurting."

And with that one sentence, spoken in his matter-of-fact voice, with his eyes so full of sympathy and understanding, she knew that she'd been wrong about what she'd seen at the fair. Reason flooded in to replace the doubt. They'd been in a public place, after all, with Paul and some other guy standing right there. She'd allowed her own self-doubt and fears to color what she'd seen with Tony and Val. Would Tony be here right now, holding her this way, if he didn't care?

"I saw you with Val," she admitted quietly. "I saw you kiss her, and I was so mad. But I was wrong."

His voice was low when he spoke. "That's what all this was about? And then you heard what your mom said and you were already upset with me?"

She nodded wordlessly. Closing her eyes, she whispered, "Yes. And then… I didn't know what to do with myself. I was so… wound up, and hurt, and angry. For so long I've been afraid you'd see who I really was, and you'd hate me. You'd push me away. I'd be too weird for you, too fucked up, and I'd never measure up as the good, normal girl you want."

He exhaled. She felt his hands on her chin, lifting her face up. His eyes were fierce and determined, when she looked at him. She'd never seen him so serious.

"You know that's all wrong, don't you?" he asked. His low voice was stern and his eyes uncompromising.

"I do," she whispered.

"Tessa," he whispered, tucking a stray strand of hair behind her ear. "We're all a little crazy. I come from a line of crazy Italians, including a grandmother everyone said was a witch." She giggled, as he continued. "But I *love* your crazy, just like you love mine. Because I love *you.*"

A lump rose in her throat, but thankfully there was no need to talk, as he bent his head down and kissed her. She tasted the salt of her tears, as his hand reached back to her neck and held her close, both hands grasping her as his mouth claimed hers. When he released her, his eyes were determined.

"You know you can trust me?" he asked quietly.

"Of course. I do, Tony. I'm so sorry."

He nodded. "And you know I love you?"

"I do," she whispered, her eyes closing briefly before opening again.

"And you still want me to do be your dom?"

Hope surged in her heart as she nodded wordlessly. He gave one determined nod as his eyes sobered and his brows furrowed. His voice dropped. "And you know I told you I would give you a *real* spanking if you ever harmed yourself."

Her stomach dropped, and her mouth grew dry, but she nodded nonetheless.

"But Nora," she whispered. "We're ordering Chinese!"

Just then, the doorbell rang, and they heard Nora's feet thumping down the hall in response.

"Fine," Tony said. "Chinese for my baby girl. *Then* the spanking she so richly deserves."

Though Tess's heart beat faster, she nodded again.

And then from down the hall came a terrifying scream.

"No word on Nora yet," Matteo said, sliding his finger across the screen of his phone to disconnect his call. "Slay is on the case and called in markers with a couple of his buddies. But it looks like your mom's boyfriend was on Salazar's payroll."

"Roger? On Salazar's payroll?" Tess repeated. "Who is Salazar? What does that even mean, Matt?"

Tess could feel Tony's fingers squeezing hers tightly, and that was the only thing keeping her from screaming the words into Matteo's grim face, even though she knew he was doing the best he could. In fact, Tony's presence next to her on the sofa had been the only thing keeping her from exploding into a million tiny shards for the past three hours, ever since she and Tony had heard Nora scream and had run from their bedroom to the living room to find the front door wide open and Nora… gone.

Through their frantic call to the police, Tony's terse call to Matteo, who had arrived within minutes, and Tess's multiple *unanswered* calls to her mother, Tony had stayed by her side. When the police officer informed her that there was little he could do *officially* given the lack of a parent or guardian to confirm that Nora was missing, and the fact that Nora was old enough to have possibly run away, Tony had wrapped his arms around her, literally and metaphorically keeping her together.

Matteo blew out a breath and answered her question. "When Tony called me earlier, the names he gave me sounded familiar. I called Slay, who called a buddy of his, and they did a little digging. Turns out the man your mother has been seeing is Roger Collier. He's mostly been a low-level lowlife up to now—one arrest for selling stolen electronics back in 2010, one in 2014 for drug possession with intent to distribute. Looks like he was selling a small amount to an undercover agent in a Burger Barn parking lot when he was arrested. Both charges dropped on technicalities."

"That's low-level?" Hillary asked angrily from Tess's other side. "Selling drugs?"

Matteo shrugged. "On the grand scale of crime? With murder and rape and kidnapping at the top of the ladder? Yeah, baby," he said softly, "that's pretty low-level."

Alice, who had arrived only fifteen minutes ago, straight from the fair, and had already taken charge by disposing of the cold, uneaten Chinese food and preparing everyone coffee, emerged from the kitchen with a tray of cookies and napkins. "But no prior history of violent crime?" she asked, setting the tray on the table next to the coffee.

She noticed everyone's attention on her and blushed. "I took a criminal psychology class in college," she explained shyly.

Matteo nodded in understanding, but then shook his head at her question. "Nah, nothing in his record that's violent. But then in the past year or so, our low-life criminal got ambitious."

"Ambitious?" Tony asked, his voice harsh with worry.

Matt nodded. "Hooked up with a guy named Gonzalo Salazar, nickname Chalo…"

"That's the guy who wanted Nora to kiss her!" Tess exclaimed.

Matt and Tony exchanged looks. Tess felt Tony nod minutely, as if granting permission for something, and then Matt spoke again.

"That doesn't surprise me, honey. Chalo Salazar is known for his fondness for underage girls."

Tess felt her stomach clench violently.

"Oh, God, Tony! This is all my fault! I should never have taunted my mother with the police. I should have seen how this…"

"Stop!" Tony told her. He squeezed her hand painfully tight for just a moment, just long enough for her to control the panic that threatened to overtake her, and catch her breath.

"Tess, if this was Salazar's doing, he probably had this plan in mind the first time he laid eyes on your sister. This isn't on you," Matt told her, his eyes on his phone screen once more. "There was nothing you could do to prevent it. And it's a damn good thing you kept your head and called us right away. Slay's *going* to find her. You need to believe it."

Tess took a deep breath and nodded.

"Heidi and Dom are on their way over," Hillary announced, looking up from the text message on her own phone. She placed her hand on Tess's knee and gave her an affectionate squeeze. "And they'll stay as long as you need them to."

"They don't have to," Tess protested.

"Of course they do," Tony said sternly. "Just like you would for them. *Family*."

Tess leaned her head on Tony's shoulder. "Okay," she agreed.

Despite her worry for Nora, she sent up a prayer of thanksgiving that Tony was there lending her his strength.

Tense moments passed while the five of them sat staring at their black phone screens, willing them to light up with new information.

What felt like hours later, Matteo's did.

"Yeah?" Matteo said excitedly into the phone. "Who? Yeah, okay. But... Slay? *Shit*. Right. Done."

As he talked, Matteo stood and walked to the intercom panel by the door, then hit the button to open the door downstairs.

He disconnected the call and turned to look at them with a relieved smile.

"They got her."

"Oh thank God. Thank *God*," Tess said, nearly sobbing with relief. Tony wrapped his arms around her and kissed the top of her head, being her rock during her happy tears just as he had been when she was half-crazy with worry, and just as she was starting to believe he might *always* be.

Seconds later, Matteo had thrown open the door, and there was Nora—looking extremely pissed off—along with a tall, muscular Hispanic man in his early twenties.

Nora's pissed off expression evaporated when she saw Tess, and she launched herself across the room into her sister's arms.

"Diego," Matt said, striding forward to shake the man's hand. "Man, I owe you."

"Nah, you don't owe me shit. She was in a storage facility over in North Bay," Diego said, his watchful eyes on Nora. "Collier took her without authorization. Trying to make sure the girl didn't talk. Chalo was, let's say, *unappreciative*, of the amount of shit about to rain down on his head. I wouldn't be surprised if Collier *left town*," he said meaningfully. "Immediate, permanent *relocation*."

Hillary winced. But as Tess hugged her sister, her eyes met Diego's deep chocolate gaze. "Thank you," she whispered to him. He lifted his chin in response.

"Don't you *thank* him," Nora protested, breaking away from Tess to glare at Diego. "He's *one of them*. One of Roger's friends!"

Diego's eyes shuttered.

"Deny it!" she accused him. "You're no better than they are. And worse. At least Roger never killed anyone!"

"Nora!" Tess cried, shocked at her sister's attitude. Then, turning to Diego, she added in a placating tone. "I'm sorry, she's obviously very upset."

Matt opened his mouth to say something but Diego shook his head once, as though in warning, and Matt remained silent.

"Nora, Diego just saved your life," Tony reminded her, his voice gentle but stern. "How about some gratitude?"

Nora's eyes locked on Diego's and her mouth remained defiantly closed.

Diego's lips twitched. "You're welcome anyway, Norita," he said softly.

Nora turned away.

"Well, I'm grateful," Tess said, shaking her head at her sister in confusion. "I don't know how we can repay you!"

Diego shrugged, as if her gratitude made him uncomfortable. "It's my job," he said shortly, exchanging another quick glance with Matteo.

Nora snorted.

Tony narrowed his eyes and opened his mouth, as though he wanted to reprimand her, but Alice interrupted.

"Um, is Slay with you?"

Diego's eyes met Matteo's again, and Matteo seemed to receive an unwritten communication, because his eyes widened in shock, then squeezed shut for a moment.

Damn these men and their silent language.

"Alex Slater was… shot," Diego finally admitted.

"What?" Hillary cried.

"Shit," Tony breathed.

"No," Alice said softly, insistently. "No. That's not right. You take me to him."

Diego looked at Matteo again, and this time the helplessness in his gaze was easy to read.

"Alice, honey," Matteo said, moving forward to put his arm around her shoulders.

Alice stepped away from him. "No, Matt. You take me to him. Someone take me to him. Now!"

Tess and Hillary exchanged a look. Neither of them had ever seen Alice so fired up and insistent.

"All right, then," Matt soothed. "That's what we'll do." His eyes sought Hillary's and he jerked his head toward the door. Hillary immediately rose to leave.

"Tell *him* I said thank you," Nora told Matteo, who frowned but nodded.

And then they left, leaving Tess holding her sister, and Tony's strong arms wrapped around both of them. A few hours ago, she'd thought she'd lost everything. But at this moment, she realized she had everything that really mattered.

Later on, once Nora had been tucked into bed and they'd heard from Matteo at the hospital to say Slay's condition had stabilized, Tony led Tess back down the hall to their bedroom, and undressed her swiftly. The room was dark but for the light of the street lamps that filtered in through the drawn curtains.

"I love you," he told her.

Tess smiled. She knew it. He'd proven it. Thank God Tony had been there to help carry her burdens, not because she wasn't *capable* of carrying them herself, but because it helped so much to know that she didn't *have* to.

"I love you, too," she said, loving the way his answering smile flashed in the gloom.

"I know you're tired, baby. I know this day has been a roller coaster for you. But do you remember where we were before all of this shit unfolded?"

She nodded. They'd had a disagreement, and she'd disobeyed him.

He pushed her hair off her face with one large hand, and led her over to the bed. He sat down, and pulled her to stand between his spread knees.

"Part of me wants to let you go to bed right now, and forget any of that ever happened. But the other part of me knows that we need to finish what we started. We need to make things right between us."

Tess's eyes sought his in the near-darkness. If she'd learned nothing else that day, it was that pushing things under the rug and refusing to deal with them didn't make them go away, it only made them fester beneath the surface. She would face him now, and do whatever he told her. She would let him make it right.

She straddled his lap, telling him without words that she agreed.

But when she was seated, he didn't immediately pull her over his lap to punish her. Instead, his eyes sought the superficial wound she'd given herself on her leg, thankfully no more than a scratch.

"Sit on the bed," he instructed. He moved her off him and walked out of the room. He returned with a washcloth and a small first aid kit, kneeling in front of her. He lifted her leg and gently dabbed the warm, dampened edge of the wash cloth on her cut. It stung, but the warmth of it was soothing. He took the dry end and patted it dry, frowning as he concentrated on getting it just right. Her heart constricted at his tender touch, as he placed a tiny drop of antibiotic on her cut before affixing a Band-Aid. When he was done, he tossed the cloth into the hamper, and turning to her, lifted her leg to his lips, kissing the sore spot.

His eyes met hers and his voice was as serious as she'd ever heard when he spoke.

"You will never do that again."

She couldn't trust herself to speak, merely nodded. He released her and stood.

"Stand, please," he said. She obeyed.

"Place your hands behind your head." She obeyed. He sat on the bed, his hands on her hips as he spun her around to face him. Swiftly, he pulled down her shorts, leaving her bare, shaking, standing before him.

"Step out of them." She did what he asked. His hands grasped her waist and he tugged her over his lap. Her belly hit his hard thighs so that she was angled, her face on the bed and her bottom perched precariously over his knee. He reached for her hand and pinned it to her lower back, as his fingers entwined with hers. The gesture was soothing, though the loss of control made her heart stutter.

"Why am I giving you a spanking, Tessa?" he asked in a low, stern voice.

"Because I cut myself," she whispered, shutting her eyes.

"After I've spanked you, we will have a good, long talk about what we're going to do to help you. Ways *I* can help you when I'm here and ways *you* can help yourself when I'm not. Understood?"

"Yes, sir." It felt nice to call him "sir," a reminder that she obeyed him and he loved her enough to take care of her in the ways she craved.

"I'm going to spank you until I think I've made my point." She felt his large hand squeeze her bare bottom. She squirmed a bit over his knee, nodding into the blanket before she felt the first sharp crack of his hand.

After that, he said very little, and she was grateful he didn't. She focused on the feeling she got as his hand descended, pausing several seconds between each hard, searing swat. Pain scattered across her naked skin as he continued spanking her, one stroke after another. After a few swats, he massaged her red-hot skin before resuming again, this time a little harder and faster. She couldn't keep count, but only focused on staying over his knee, as little by little he stripped her of the layers of emotions. All she could focus on was lying across his lap. The second time he paused, rubbing her sore bottom, he began to lecture.

"I don't *ever* want to have to do this again, not like this, and not for this reason," he said, before delivering the hardest swat he'd ever given her. "You're beautiful. You're strong. You're resilient." He raised his hand, punctuating each word with a stinging stroke of his palm. "And *you. Are. Mine.*"

A sob rent through her then, at the knowledge that she was his and he loved her, and he didn't love some fake Tessa he didn't know, but the *real* woman, the wounded woman who was strong, and capable, who worked hard and loved deeply and would face her struggles head on. He loved her, the crazy and the silly, the sexy and the smart. He loved everything about her but they would make it work, because *they were worth it*.

He gave her two more stinging swats. And then he was done spanking her. He quickly divested her of what little clothing remained. He had her flat on her back on the bed as she cried, and his mouth met hers.

"I love you, Tessa," he whispered, his hands frantically reaching for the edge of his t-shirt and yanking it up over his head. She felt light, then, as if all that weighed her down had been lifted. She was here, alone, with the man who knew her and loved her anyway, and *she loved him back*. Her hands went to his waist at the same time his did. Laughing, they fumbled together until they were both bared to one another. He nestled down on her, holding his weight up just enough so that he didn't harm her, but she still felt every inch of him on her as his knee spread her legs and he entered her.

"Hell yeah," she groaned, as he filled her, his hips grinding into her unapologetically, and she welcomed every fierce stroke. Her ass was on fire from the spanking, her mind cleared and peaceful, and now her body hummed with need.

"God I want you so bad," she moaned.

"You've got me, baby," he said, and for some reason that made her laugh out loud, because how much more of him could she have when he'd just spanked her and kissed her and told her he loved her, and now they were stark naked, making love?

He smacked her ass when she laughed, which made her need intensify, and then he was groaning, her own climax right on the cusp behind his.

"We're a crazy couple," she said, as his head fell to her chest and she ran her hands through his hair, admiring his broad shoulders and husky form, spent, atop her.

"Loco," he agreed. "Stark raving mad." Then he lifted himself up on an elbow, placing his chin in his hand and gazing at her. "Now are you gonna behave yourself? I'm getting tired. This is kind of a lot of work, this dom thing."

"I'll be good… for now. All right, big guy?"

He grinned, bringing her fingers to his lips with a kiss. "That's my girl."

Epilogue

Tony opened the oven and peeked in at the bubbling, cheesy goodness that was his Nana Angelico's famous lasagna. Just a few more minutes, in his expert opinion, until it was perfect and ready for the Thanksgiving table, along with the turkey and other fixings that were waiting on the counter.

"Hope I got it right, Nana," he said under his breath.

From the living room came the roar of an excited crowd.

"What happened?" Tony called to the group assembled around the TV as he walked over to perch on the arm of the loveseat next to Tess. "Someone score?"

"Yup! Another touchdown for the Cowboys!" Matteo announced from his chair, punching one tattooed arm in the air. "I'm so winning the over-under for this quarter!" His smile was wide, victorious, and just a tiny bit smug.

"Dream on," Dom told him from the other side of the living room, where he was snuggled down in the sofa with Heidi's head on his chest. "There's still seven minutes left, and Warner's back on the field." He stroked a hand down Heidi's back and held her more firmly to him.

"Is Warner the one with the dimples who does the pizza ad?" Hillary asked from her spot on the floor by Matteo's legs as she reached over and grabbed an olive from the antipasto platter on the coffee table. Her waving hair was now back to its natural rich auburn color… which was apparently meaningful and symbolic somehow, or so Tess had told him. Tony was having trouble getting used to the change, but Matt seemed to embrace it wholeheartedly, if the look he gave his girl was any indication.

"Nah, I think he's the one with the shaving cream ad," Nora corrected as she sprawled on the rug in front of the TV, perfectly at ease with the family who had adopted her and enfolded her into their ranks. "And the amazing abs."

"Ooh, speaking of abs! The other night Dom was watching some show on TV, and there were a bunch of half-naked football players just kinda standing around a locker room in skimpy towels, smiling and winking at each other. The abs were *hypnotizing*," Heidi told them dreamily, sitting forward to grab her beer.

"What show was *this*?" John demanded from the dining room, as he put the final touches on the beautiful centerpiece he'd crafted. "And why have I not been watching it?"

"Jesus," Paul muttered from the couch, rolling his eyes at his boyfriend. John shrugged sheepishly and Paul shook his head, but his eyes danced. Then he turned to Dom and joked, "So you've been letting our girl watch porn, Dom?"

Tessa snickered. Tony shot her a mock-glare that made her clap her hands over her mouth in an effort to be quiet, even as she giggled harder.

"If by 'our girl' you mean '*my wife*,' and by porn you mean ESPN's Sports Report, then yeah," Dom agreed dryly. "Guilty."

Tony burst into laughter along with the rest of the crew, including Heidi herself.

"Whatever!" she said, poking Dom in the ribs. "You're busy

listening to what they're saying, but if you just sat back and admired the visual, you'd see it was *hot*."

"Matteo, maybe *we* need to watch Sports Report!" Hillary teased, leaning her chin on his knee.

"Damn it, Tinker Bell! I had this fantasy where you asked me to turn the channel to sports news," Matt groused. "And you've just ruined it. Now I'll always be wondering if you're just watching for the hypnotizing abs. I'm not even gonna be able to watch Sports Report until football season is over!"

Hillary pouted.

Dom snickered.

"Bro, *this* is the shit you fantasize about?" Tony demanded, shaking his head in mock sympathy. "Ooh, Matt, you're so sexy! Now turn the channel to Sports Report!" he said, falsetto voice.

"Shut up!" Matt said, balling up a napkin and lobbing it at Tony's head as everyone laughed. "I didn't say that was the *whole* fantasy!"

"There's always hockey season!" Nora consoled Hillary, sitting up to pat her knee. "Those players are rugged and *built*! They make football players look like sissies."

Matt scowled at the two women. "We'll wait till spring," he announced.

Nora shrugged and arched a teasing eyebrow. "That's fine. Baseball players wear those tight little…"

"Can you control this kid, Tony?" Matt demanded as Nora and Hillary giggled.

Tony snorted. Control Nora, the whip-smart firecracker who had absolutely blossomed since coming to live with Tess and him a few weeks ago and getting her early acceptance to Boston University? Who had shown no signs of lasting trauma from her abduction, according to the psychologist, and was already looking forward to a career in social work, making life better for other kids who grew up like she had? No way. And he'd kill any motherfucker who tried.

"That lasagna smells delicious already," Tess said softly, beaming up at him.

He leaned over and pressed a kiss to her luscious mouth. He couldn't help it. And then, because she tasted like cherry lip gloss and happiness, he did it again.

"Hey, knock it off!" Matt called. "There are children present!"

Nora raised an eyebrow. "My birthday was last week, remember?"

Matt rolled his eyes. "Well, I wasn't referring to *you*, obviously, since you're a newly-minted eighteen-year-old *adult*. I mean, there *will* be a child when Alice and Charlie come over for dessert."

Nora shook her head, but smiled.

Tony leaned back, but his eyes held Tessa's warm brown ones. "Love you," he said, so low that only she could hear. She closed her eyes for just a second, like she was overcome, and when she opened them, they almost glowed.

"Love you, too, Tony. So much."

"Gag!" Nora yelled from the floor, burying her face in her hands. "I'm suddenly thinking Matt's right. Young, impressionable *child* right *here*!"

Tony rolled his eyes, but leaned back and entwined his fingers with Tess's instead. "Too late to turn back now, kiddo. Remember you gave me a whole speech last week about how adults didn't need curfews?"

"Not that you *listened*," Nora complained. "You told me I still have to be home by twelve on weekends unless I'm at the restaurant with you."

Tony nodded. *Damn straight.*

"I have the strictest parents-who-aren't-parents of anyone I know," Nora said with a sigh.

Despite the sigh, Tony noted that she didn't seem particularly upset about this.

"Nothing good happens after midnight," Tony informed her with another firm nod.

"Holy shit!" Dom laughed, throwing his head back into the seat.

"Oh my God!" Matt crowed, his green eyes wide and staring. "You just... you just..."

"I just what?" Tony demanded, scowling.

"You just completely channeled Mom!" Dom said. His eyes were crinkled with humor. "She used to say that exact thing to us. Well, usually to Matt..."

"You want to stay out until the middle of the night, Matteo?" Matt said, his voice taking on their mother's thick Italian accent. "For what? Good girls are home by eleven-thirty because they know nothing good happens after midnight!"

Oh. *Oh, God.* She *had* said that. Tony had officially become his mother.

Beside him, Tess collapsed with laughter.

"Oh, Tony, the look on your face!" she giggled.

Tony shook his head. "Well, she had a point," he argued.

"She did!" Dom agreed in his deep voice. "That's why I make sure *my* good girl is always home by eleven-thirty... unless she's with me." Heidi propped herself up on his chest and touched her lips to his.

"Aw," John said, his eyes on Dom and Heidi as he moved to the sofa to sit next to Paul. "You guys are too cute." Paul put his arm around John's shoulders.

"I don't know about the 'nothing good happening after midnight' part, though," Matt mused, smirking down at Hillary and deliberately waggling his eyebrows. "Pretty sure she got *that* wrong. Because just last night..."

Hillie's eyes grew wide and she smacked his leg in outrage. "Matteo!"

"Jesus," Dom said in disgust.

"Lalalala, don't want to know!" Heidi chanted, blocking her ears.

Matteo laughed long and unrepentantly.

"Well, I'm gonna take *my* good girl to the kitchen to get her away from all you lunatics," Tony said, standing and pulling Tess along by their clasped hands.

"Need some help?" Nora offered.

"Nah! You all helped enough earlier. Just waiting for the last couple things," Tony told her with a wink. "Relax, kiddo."

"Yeah, come sit by Uncle John and we'll watch the sexy men on TV jump on top of each other," John told Nora, making her laugh.

"Lunatics!" Tony repeated, wrapping his arm around Tess's waist and steering her toward the kitchen.

"But they're really *nice* lunatics," Tess told him when they reached the kitchen. "All of us are."

Tony smiled. They were. The very best kind of lunatics. But that wasn't why he smiled.

A month or two ago, he couldn't have imagined Tess making that statement. But thanks to the weekly therapy sessions she'd been receiving at Mass General, Tess no longer worried that her urges to cut made her "crazy."

"Doctor Elaine says it's a fairly common coping mechanism, especially among younger women and girls. She sees it a lot in her practice. It's just something I have to deal with," Tess had told him with obvious relief after her second session with the kink-friendly therapist who another submissive at The Club had recommended. "I have a lot of issues with repressing emotion. But now that I'm in a safe environment and getting the help I need, it'll be a lot easier for me to deal with them in a healthy way."

And Tony would do whatever it took to make sure that his girl always knew she was safe with him… and loved, no matter what.

"Have you heard from Slay?" Tess asked suddenly. "Is he coming tonight?"

Tony shook his head. "I haven't heard much from him since he got out of the hospital. Matt says he's already back at the gym on light duty." He rolled his eyes and Tess grinned. "We need to get that guy some carbs. Maybe Matt can drag him to *Cara*. We'll have to *make him an offer he can't refuse.*"

Tess rolled her eyes. "Stick to the lasagna, Brando," she joked.

As Tess moved the roasted vegetables to one thick white platter, Tony carved the turkey onto another. Then Tess began moving the platters of food to the huge table, and Tony checked the lasagna one last time.

Perfectly golden brown, exactly the way Nana had always made it.

He carried it to the table and put it in a place of honor just as everyone took their seats.

"Oh, Tony, that smells incredible!" Hillary said, inhaling deeply. "We never did lasagna on Thanksgiving when I was growing up."

"We had no idea what we were missing!" Heidi said, her eyes on the dish.

"Speaking of which… I wonder what Mom and Dad are up to right now," Hillary said, looking at Heidi with comically wide eyes.

"I can't believe they chose to go on a cruise over Thanksgiving rather than spend it with us!" Heidi sniffed.

"I can't believe they chose to spend Thanksgiving *together* in the first place!" Hillary exclaimed.

"I'm not," Matteo said. He helped himself to potatoes and passed the bowl to Paul, who was sitting next to him. "I've always suspected that two people who claimed to dislike each other the way your parents did must still love each other deep down."

"*Way* deep down, maybe," Heidi said dubiously, dishing

stuffing onto her plate. "If you'd ever heard them fight over her political protests… Mom rants and throws plates, Dad glares at her and starts attacking her arguments point by point. Neither one of them will give in, and it goes on for hours."

"Well, but that's the thing, isn't it?" Dom said gently. "He pays attention to her. He's focused on her. He shows her she's important."

"By arguing with her?" Nora was skeptical.

"By not giving in," Paul corrected.

Nora seemed thoughtful, but John nodded. "I can see that. If he didn't care, he wouldn't engage her the way he does."

"Exactly. He's concerned about her safety and that she's using poor judgment. He doesn't want her to get hurt," Paul said. "It's just… harder for him to express that than it is for, um… certain other people." He gave Heidi a significant look, as though he didn't want to explain more plainly in front of Nora.

Heidi nodded. "Maybe they'll figure out a new way of communicating, then. That'd be something to be thankful for."

Dom smiled. "One of many things this year," he reminded her.

And Tony realized how true it was. Last Thanksgiving, he and Dom and Matt had spent dinner with their aunt's boisterous family, but it hadn't felt right somehow. Despite the warmth and welcome they'd received, they'd felt like outsiders. Other. Not fully known or included. But this year…

"Hey!" Nora said, just as they picked up their forks to eat. "Nobody said grace!"

Matteo paused with a forkful of turkey in his mouth and swallowed sheepishly. "Oh. Right."

"How about a toast instead?" John offered. "To being loved!" He looked at Paul and smiled.

"To being *adored*," Paul said, his voice deep and his eyes shining.

"To being known," Hillary said, her eyes on Matteo. "Sometimes better than you know yourself."

"To being accepted." Heidi quirked an eyebrow at Dom. "No matter what."

"To trust," Matt said. "And being worthy of it."

"To being safe," Nora said softly.

"To working hard, working *together*," Dom added.

"To family," Tess said, smiling at Tony.

Tony felt some choking, unmanly emotion tighten his chest, so he couldn't add another thing... but that was okay, because Tess had really said it all.

Silence reigned for a time while everyone savored the food, but after a moment, Dom piped up. "Best lasagna ever, brother. You've done Nana Angelico proud."

Tony nodded, then sent a kiss to the heavens for the woman who had taught them to value good food, and family, and true love.

They had *all* done her proud.

The End

Jane Henry

USA Today bestselling author Jane Henry pens stern but loving alpha heroes, feisty heroines, and emotion-driven happily-ever-afters. She writes what she loves to read: kink with a tender touch. Jane is a hopeless romantic who lives on the East Coast with a houseful of children and her very own Prince Charming.

Don't miss these exciting titles by Jane Henry and Blushing Books!

A Thousand Yesses

Bound to You series
Begin Again, Book 1
Come Back To Me, Book 2
Complete Me, Book 3

Boston Doms Series
By Jane Henry and Maisy Archer
My Dom, Book 1
His Submissive, Book 2
Her Protector, Book 3
His Babygirl, Book 4
His Lady, Book 5
Her Hero, Book 6
My Redemption, Book 7

Anthologies

Hero Undercover
Sunstrokes

Connect with Jane Henry
janehenrywriter.blogspot.com
janehenrywriter@gmail.com

Maisy Archer

Maisy is an unabashed book nerd who has been in love with romance since reading her first Julie Garwood novel at the tender age of 12. After a decade as a technical writer, she finally made the leap into writing fiction several years ago and has never looked back. Like her other great loves - coffee, caramel, beach vacations, yoga pants, and her amazing family - her love of words has only continued to grow... in a manner inversely proportional to her love of exercise, house cleaning, and large social gatherings. She loves to hear from fellow romance lovers, and is always on the hunt for her next great read.

Don't miss these exciting titles by Jane Henry and Maisy Archer with Blushing Books!

Boston Doms Series
By Jane Henry and Maisy Archer
My Dom, Book 1
His Submissive, Book 2
Her Protector, Book 3
His Babygirl, Book 4
His Lady, Book 5
Her Hero, Book 6
My Redemption, Book 7

Anthologies
Hero Undercover
Sunstrokes

Connect with Maisy Archer
janeandmaisy.com

Blushing Books

Blushing Books is one of the oldest eBook publishers on the web. We've been running websites that publish spanking and BDSM related romance and erotica since 1999, and we have been selling eBooks since 2003. We hope you'll check out our hundreds of offerings at http://www.blushingbooks.com.